KINKY

JUSTINE ELYOT

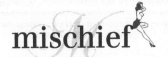

Mischief
An imprint of HarperCollins*Publishers*
77–85 Fulham Palace Road,
Hammersmith, London W6 8JB

www.mischiefbooks.com

A Paperback Original 2013

First published in Great Britain in ebook format by
HarperCollins*Publishers* 2012

Copyright © Justine Elyot 2012

Justine Elyot asserts the moral right to
be identified as the author of this work

A catalogue record for this book is
available from the British Library

ISBN-13: 9780007534739

Set in Sabon by FMG using Atomic ePublisher from Easypress

Find out more about HarperCollins and the environment at
www.harpercollins.co.uk/green

CONTENTS

CONTENTS

Chapter One

There's a place further down the street where I work that I can't figure out at all. From the outside, it looks like your standard Shoreditch warehouse converted into an 'art space', the Victorian brickwork decorated in multi-coloured swirls and curls, but so many people come in and go out of its heavily fortified black entrance that I think there must be more to it than that.

And there seems to be some kind of door policy too. For every half-dozen people who are admitted, another four or five are turned away. From my desk at the ad agency, I watch the ebb and flow.

'I reckon it's a brothel,' says Anton, breaking from *Angry Birds* for a moment to look out of the window with me.

'But there are just as many women visiting as men.'

'A bisexual brothel, then.'

'I don't think it's a brothel,' I say, but I'm not so sure he's wrong. Although the visitors vary wildly in age, sex and appearance, rather a lot of them seem to be dressed to impress. I've seen a woman in full rubber body stocking and spike heels go in there with a man in a Savile Row suit. Another time, a man was actually carrying a bull-whip. One gorgeous young guy crawled along the pavement from the corner with a collar and leash attached to his neck. The woman 'walking' him looked like a retired librarian. It's odd and fascinating. My money's on a private sex club, but it seems to open all hours rather than late at night, and most of the people who enter look no different from the average collection of Joes on my morning commute.

Anton's attention reverts to his smartphone. 'Get in,' he says. 'Just got a text from Riley – she's got free tickets to a secret DJ Mentallist gig at the Fish Bowl. You up for it?'

'Ohhh.' I half-rise from my seat and then plonk myself back down, glumness personified. 'Can't. Really got to finish this campaign. Looks like I'm going to be pulling a late one. Sorry.'

Anton shrugs. 'No biggie, blood.'

He likes to try and sound like a mockney version of someone out of *The Wire*, but Anton is actually the privately educated son of a brigadier.

I wave at his retreating figure and gaze down at my chaotic notepad. If I don't come up with a slogan for this bastard air freshener by the end of the evening, I'm sunk. Maybe 'This will freshen your bastard air'. It's better than the crap I'm coming up with at the moment, at least. 'Give your nose a break'. Ugh.

I hunker down and try to clear my mind, not an easy task when your mental clutter could fill a mental landfill site.

Some time around eight, I happen to look up from the catchphrase nightmare and notice something different about the Building of Enigma.

I hurry over to the window and squint through the blinds. Running along the bottom of the wall, barely above pavement level, are a series of narrow barred windows, slim rectangles with their long sides parallel to the ground. I've often tried to peer into them in passing but found them blacked out and impenetrable.

Tonight, one of them glows with light.

Abandoning the bastard air freshener, I grab my bag and head for the lifts, my feet hardly touching the ground.

Outside, the darkened street is deserted – or so I think. Before I can cross to the object of my curiosity, a hand touches my shoulder and I swing around, irritated and slightly nervous. This isn't the safest area of town, the classic price you pay for being edgy and hip.

'Scuse me, you have a light?'

The voice is foreign, the speaker dressed in a way that places him somewhere between art student and gypsy, all leather bracelets and ripped jeans. The thing that really captures my attention, though, is his amazing moustache. You don't see facial hair like that except in yellowed photographs of Victorian military men. I'm so struck by it that I forget to answer for a moment, until he makes a flourish with his hand, drawing my eye to his unlit cigarette.

'No?' he says.

'Um, no, sorry,' I say, wanting him to go away so I can spy in peace. I feel awkward going over to the building and blatantly rubbernecking in front of a stranger.

'OK,' he says. 'You know where is a bar?'

'God, there are hundreds round here. Just walk in any direction.'

I turn to cross the street, tense with the idea that somebody might put the blackout blind back down at any moment. Sod this random tourist. I'm going to get my answer to the mystery that has plagued me since I joined Cre8iv back in the spring.

'Why you are unfriendly to me?'

Oh God, just go away! He is following me across the street, his voice plaintive, his belts jangling. How many does a man need anyway?

'All English girls are like this?'

I reach my target and crouch on the pavement, getting myself into optimum peeking position.

4

Kinky

'Please stop harassing me,' I snap, then I take a huge lungful of toxic London air and fail to find any more words until a heartfelt 'Oh my God!' escapes my lips.

'You are OK?'

The tourist guy kneels down next to me. I try to flap him away with my shaking hand, but he is having none of it. He leans forwards, wanting to see what it is that has shocked me so.

'Wow,' he says, sounding impressed. 'This is typical London bar?' He chuckles. 'The English vice, right?'

'Uh-huh.' I can't speak, I'm too engrossed in what I'm witnessing.

We are looking down into a plain, cell-like basement room. The exposed brickwork is painted white and bare of decoration. A bank of four old-fashioned school desks take up the central space, while facing us at the end is a chalkboard with some Latin verb conjugations written on it. The verb of the day appears to be *Flagello* – to flagellate. Very apposite, given that the stern-looking middle-aged man standing beside the board is wielding a crook-handled cane of the type that was banned in schools when I was a wee girl.

At three of the four desks, their backs to us, sit two overgrown schoolboys and an overgrown schoolgirl. I had no idea you could get school uniforms in adult sizes but obviously there's a niche market out there.

At the front, beside the 'teacher', a woman of about

5

thirty, pigtailed and mini-kilted, stands on a chair with her hands on her head. She is trembling a little, her face is flushed, but it's unclear whether fear or excitement predominates in her emotions. I suppose it must be excitement, given that the sight of her in her humiliating predicament is making my stomach squirm a little and my knickers dampen. I try to attune myself to what might be going through her mind and find myself surprisingly keen to experience it at firsthand.

I hold my breath, then let it out when the teacher lifts the hem of her skirt with the tip of his cane, revealing the kind of navy-blue gym knickers that went out in about 1975. She is made to hold the skirt up and turn around, giving the class an eyeful of her full, rounded bum.

The teacher says something, swishing his cane through the air, and she steps off the chair, carefully, hands still on head, then she bends and places her palms flat on the seat, sticking out that arse so that the gym knickers stretch and outline it in pitiless detail.

The teacher addresses his pupils, punctuating his words by smacking the hand that isn't holding the cane down on the disgraced girl's bottom repeatedly. Her flesh quivers but she keeps her position. How painful is it? I wish I could hear through the heavy glazing. I want to know what that sounds like.

He stops and says something to the girl, who stands

and then peels down her knickers to her knees. My breathing is ragged as the freshly spanked pink globes are revealed to shameful view. God, what must she be thinking and feeling? If she's anything like me, she'll be soaking wet around the crotch. I've had this kind of fantasy for years, but never expected to see it in action.

She reassumes the position, sticking her arse out at the teacher's injunction and spreading her legs wide enough for me to be able to see, even at this distance, that she is aroused. Doesn't it bother her that everyone can see?

I want to put my hand down my skirt, but the inconvenient presence of tourist guy thwarts me. For his part, his eyes are on stalks, his long nose almost butting the bars in his eagerness to get the best view. What a voyeur. Yes, I'm a hypocrite.

The teacher flexes his cane then positions himself at a suitable distance from his victim's well-presented derrière and draws back his weapon.

He holds it there for so long that my chest begins to ache with expectant tension. Then he flicks his wrist, the cane blurs through the air and makes contact with her bottom. I flinch, and so does she.

'Ouch,' says tourist guy.

A line of white appears on her skin, then it turns redder and redder until she has a magnificent scarlet welt across the broad centre of her arse. It looks wildly painful.

I want to know how wildly painful it is. And I want tourist guy to fuck off so I can masturbate whilst contemplating this. But that's going to have to wait until I'm in my bed, I suppose.

The teacher lays six strokes in total, and the girl somehow miraculously stays in position, though she flexes her feet and bobs up and down after each cruel blow. She is made to kiss the rod while I admire the gorgeous pattern of red stripes she bears on her bum for all to see.

Teacher tucks her skirt into her waistband so she can't hide her punished condition and makes her stand back on the chair, while he turns back to the board and the conjugation of Latin verbs.

Then, disastrously, he looks up, directly at us, and freezes in horror before opening a door and bellowing something out of it.

'Shit!'

In my haste to back away, I fall on my behind on the pavement. The massive black door is opening, the security staff on their way out.

Tourist guy yanks me up by the elbow. 'Come on,' he urges, taking to his heels and running with me to the end of the street and into the council estate beyond, dodging around the blocks at breakneck speed. He has long legs and apparently superhuman stamina, and my heart is banging fit to explode from my chest by the time we hit the nearest pub and take refuge inside, me wheezing, him laughing.

'What's funny?' I pant, sinking on to a banquette, staring at him.

He has a crazy laugh. He looks crazy all round. What the hell I'm doing in a pub with him after watching a live sex show I just don't know.

'This is funny! I am in London three hours and I love it already. Is it like this always?'

'Not really.' I regain some rhythm to my breathing. 'Well, a bit, maybe. Shit, do you think they saw our faces? I work in the building opposite. I don't want to be recognised.'

'Don't worry. What do you drink?'

'I could murder a stiff vodka and tonic.'

'Ah, vodka. I like you. Right, stay there, I buy.'

I watch him go to the bar. He has this swagger about him, and he obviously charms the pants off the barmaid, who giggles and blushes her way through the transaction. At one point he leans forwards to let her touch his moustache. What a tart. Why am I even in this pub with him? I should just go home, but I feel the need to deconstruct what just happened, and nobody else would understand, so I stay.

He comes back with two tumblers of vodka and one bottle of tonic, setting them down with a flourish. He seats himself opposite me and flashes me a crooked smile.

'This is great,' he says. 'This morning I am in shitty apartment in Moscow and now I am in London pub with a nice girl. Thank you to my good luck.'

'You're Russian,' I say, finding it a little odd that I'm making small talk with a man I just watched a kinky schoolroom scene alongside. Should we not maybe mention it?

He thrusts out an arm. 'Dimitri,' he says. He offers a hand to shake, or so I think. When I put mine in his, he raises it to his lips and kisses it. I am so undone by this that I forget to tell him my name until he prompts me.

'Rosie,' I tell him, somewhat reluctantly.

'English Rosie,' he says with a charming smile. When you look at him properly, he's actually quite cute even if his style suggests his life is one long Glastonbury Festival. His eyes are an amazing steely blue and the moustache deflects attention away from cheekbones you could cut yourself on. Plus there's something endearing about his enthusiasm and confidence. He has the air of a man who loves life and is determined to live it. That's not so common in a city full of achingly self-conscious hipsters. It's attractive.

I eye him over the rim of my vodka glass, wondering where the evening will go. It slipped out of my grasp long ago and now I feel that all I can do is let it take its own course.

'So,' I say, unable to avoid the topic any longer, 'this is turning out to be quite an, er, interesting evening.'

'Interesting, yes. I have questions. Many questions. First – what happens next?'

'Next?' I don't quite understand what he means. 'We drink our vodka?'

'No, with those people. That man beats that girl. What are they doing now?'

'I've no idea! I guess he repeats the experience with the other three.'

'You don't know? Don't you watch them before?'

'No! I've never seen it. It's the first time they've left the blind up. That's why I wanted to watch – because I wanted to know what was going on in there.'

'Really? So it's not because you are a pervert?'

I spill my vodka. 'No!'

'Hey, hey, calm, relax. I don't want to insult you. I think you enjoyed the show, that's all.'

My face flares into fiery heat. Was it that obvious? I can't look at his sly grin, and I can't think of an answer.

'It's OK,' he says, after a few seconds of silence. 'I enjoyed it too. Why not? It's just a bit of sexy fun, right? Oh, now you are embarrassed. I don't mean to embarrass you.'

One slender finger touches my cheek, brushing it tenderly. A high-voltage shot of desire streaks down to my groin. Fuck. I think I fancy this freak show of a dude.

11

'This is just too weird,' I mutter. 'I don't know what I think.'

'You don't have to be shame,' he says. 'Everyone has their little different what's the word?'

'Quirks? Kinks?'

'Kinks. Right. You like this spanking kink, no shame.'

'I think shame is kind of the whole point.'

'Oh, OK! You like to be shame! I get it.'

'Why am I discussing my sexual preferences with you?'

'Because you like me. Anyway, what happens next in there? You think they all are spanked. Do you think it becomes sexual? Does he fuck them?'

'What, all four of them? I doubt it.'

'True, four in a row is hard. But possible.'

He winks at me and I slap the air in front of his face. What a cheeky bastard this man is. What a sexy cheeky bastard.

'Maybe they all have an orgy on the desks. I haven't got a clue.'

'You think they pay him? Or he pays them?'

'Oh, perhaps. Or they could just be like-minded friends who get together and play ye olde boarding schools every third Wednesday of the month. I guess that happens.'

'Hmm.' Dimitri's eyes cloud over for a few moments and I watch him lose himself in thought. I start to wonder about him. Who the hell is he and what is his purpose in coming to London? Is he as mad, bad and dangerous to know as the vibe he emits suggests? 'You see, Rosie, I need work. I need money. I think I could beat some asses for a living. Easy, no problem. And I will enjoy it too. Better than working in some kitchen, right?'

'I'm not sure the market for that kind of thing is exactly huge,' I demur, and then I break off and hide my face with the food menu because the 'teacher' and his four pupils have just walked through the door.

'Hey, great, I can ask him!' exclaims Dimitri, ignoring my wail of 'Fuck, no!' He springs out of his seat to confront our new acquaintances.

I follow him, trying to stop him, but I am too late. I hide my face in my hands and utter desperate prayers while he accosts the teacher.

'Excuse me, I am new in town and I have a question.'

'Oh, really?' The teacher sounds wary, but he doesn't seem to recognise us, which is some scant comfort.

'Where is good fetish club in London?'

Silence.

'Oh my God,' I mutter into my hands.

'Is this some kind of joke?'

'No joke, I promise. I like to spank girls back home in Russia and I am requiring this service in London, is possible you can help me?'

I really think I might die of cringing.

'Shall we drink elsewhere tonight?' The teacher addresses his flock. 'I can't cope with lunatics just now.' He turns stiffly and leads his pupils out of the pub.

'Great. Nice work,' I snipe. 'What the actual fuck are you on?'

'Hey, you like shame, I give you shame. What's wrong with that?'

I am seriously contemplating calling an emergency taxi when the door of the pub opens again and the girl who was caned, pigtails still bobbing, slips in and tiptoes up to us.

'Sorry about him,' she says, cheeks pink. 'But if you want to know the best place in London for BDSM and fetish, it's actually just around the corner from here.'

'Oh yes?' Dimitri leans towards her and she seems to quiver like an aspen. Oh God. He obviously has this effect on all women.

'It's called Kinky Cupcake, but you can't just go in. You have to know the password. It's members only.'

'How you get to be a member?'

'You make friends with another member. I'll be your friend if you like.'

'I will like that a lot.' His voice is all low and seductive, bloody man-whore that he is.

She giggles. 'OK, tell the doorman that Trixietots sent you. The password is Lacoste.'

'Trixietots. Lacoste. Right.'

'Have fun. Maybe I'll see you in there sometime. I really ought to go now, or Mr Strict will wonder where I am. And I don't want to make him angry, believe me.'

She giggles again, flutters her eyelashes and flees.

'Does this happen to you a lot?' I ask, curling my lip. 'Random women throwing themselves at you?'

'You are jealous?'

'No! But you love it, don't you? You're a man-whore.'

'Man-whore? A gigolo? I could do that. I am very good at the sex.'

I give up. This man's relationship with shame is utterly opposite to my own.

'Come on, let's go,' he urges and drains his vodka.

'Go?'

'Yes, to this place, of course. Kinky Cupcake. You want to see inside, don't you?'

Of course I do. Of course.

But now? And with him?

'They won't let us in. Or they might let you in, but probably not me. You're the one old Trixietots there was interested in.'

'Stop make excuses. What are you afraid of?'

'I'm not afraid.'

'Yes you are. I know why you're afraid. You may have to be honest about your, what was it, your kinks. You're scared of your kinks, right?'

'Wrong.'

He shakes his head, giving me a look of disapproval that makes me see exactly how good he'd be as a stern teacher type. Very good. Blinding.

My legs buckle. Suddenly I just want him so badly I could ...

'You want this,' he says, bending down to speak the words into my ear. 'Here is your chance to get what you want. Take it.'

'Don't leave me in there,' I whisper. 'Stay with me.'

'I'll stay with you, I promise.'

He takes my hand and walks with me back across the estate and into the street where I work. The office lights are all out now, but it's too late to panic about the air-freshener campaign. I have a new campaign on my mind.

I hold on tight as he knocks on that oft-regarded door.

It opens a fraction.

'Password,' demands a disembodied voice.

'Lacoste,' says Dimitri.

The door opens.

'Sign the members' book,' says a black-suited man, but as he looks at us he frowns. 'Are you new?'

'Trixietots recommended us,' I tell him.

'Both of you?'

I nod, hoping upon hope that this will be accepted.

'Which of you is the dom and which the sub?'

I blink, understanding neither of these terms.

'Or are you switches?'

Switches?

'She likes for me to whip her,' says Dimitri helpfully, and I kick him rather violently in the ankle, though he seems not to register. 'Don't you, Rosie?'

'Yeah.'

'Tell them,' he insists. 'Say the words.'

Oh God, you bastard!

The doorman laughs. 'I get the picture.' He hands a blue badge to Dimitri. 'You're the dom.' My badge is red. 'You're the sub. Now hold on there a minute and I'll call up Mal and O. They're the owners – they'll want to vet you.'

'Vet us?'

He nods, the phone already at his ear while he waits for the other end to pick up. 'Yeah, Mal, I've got a couple of newbies here. You got a minute to come and do the necessary? Great. I'll show them up.'

We follow him up some narrow stairs and through a door that leads to a little waiting room. It would almost be like a dentist's waiting room, if the magazines didn't feature cover models in latex and the pictures on the wall were of rotting teeth instead of people tied up with their rude bits on show. The pot plants and the water cooler give an incongruous everyday feel to what I am sure will not be an everyday experience.

'They won't be a moment,' says the doorman. 'I'll get

back downstairs now, if you don't mind. Had a bit of an incident earlier with vanillas trying to spy on us – better make sure everything's clear.'

Once he is gone, I turn to Dimitri. 'Vanillas? I feel like I'm learning a whole new vocabulary here.'

He squeezes my hand. 'Think of me. I am learning English too.'

'I feel a bit nervous. What are they going to do? What's this vetting?'

He puts an arm around my shoulder. God, it feels nice. I would be happy just to sit there like that for the rest of the evening.

'Don't worry. It's an adventure. Enjoy it.'

That seems to be his philosophy of life, I muse. I snuggle into his side and he rubs his fingers soothingly up and down my upper arm. He smells of so many things – cigarette smoke, wood smoke, mint, something herbal a bit like a joss stick. I breathe him in, inhaling intoxication.

The spell is broken when a door beyond the waiting room opens and a man dressed up as a vampire beckons us in.

I look askance at Dimitri, but he appears to be qualm-free, striding into the office with that snake-hipped swagger I had admired earlier.

Sitting behind a desk is a woman in a very smart 1940s-style skirt suit and a pillbox hat with a veil.

18

'Good evening,' says the vampire, putting out a hand for us to shake. 'I'm Mal, and this is O. We're the people behind Kinky Cupcake – we own the lot of you.' He laughs. 'You're new here, I gather, so we need to run through a few things with you. Nothing to worry about – we just have to make sure all new members are genuine deviants, if you like. It'd be a shame if a journalist or somebody unfriendly to our interests slipped through the net and ruined what we've got here, don't you think?'

'Sure.' Dimitri nods vigorously. I offer a weak smile.

'So I'm going to run through the dos and don'ts of the club with you, and then I just need a little demonstration of your dynamic, if you don't mind. I gather you, sir, are the dom and this lovely lady is your sub, so perhaps you could show us how you like to spank her, or a bit of bondage maybe ...'

What? My mouth falls open and I stare at Dimitri, aghast.

'Ah, don't be shy now,' pipes up O in a sexy husky voice. 'We've all seen it a thousand times. You'll see me whipped by every dom in the place before too long. But I know the first time in front of other people is hard, so please be aware that I sympathise. I envy you too. Gosh, that feeling of being on the edge of a precipice – the exhilaration. I'd give anything to relive that, you lucky thing.'

'If you're really not ready, I can get him to spank O instead,' offers Mal, but I shake my head.

No. If he touches any woman's bottom, it will be mine.

'No, no,' I croak. 'It's fine. I'll do it.'

I'll do it.

Chapter Two

The first rule of kink club, apparently, is that you don't talk about kink club. There are other rules too, centring on respect and consent – basic good manners, I guess. You don't strip people naked and whip them unless they want you to. You take turns. You play nicely.

I find myself watching Mal's lips as he enunciates. He has blue lipstick on and his false vampire teeth are fascinating to follow. Perhaps they aren't even false. Perhaps he's had them filed that way.

I come to with a slight jerk of the neck when O asks us a direct question. What do we do for a living?

'I'm in advertising,' I tell her.

'Oh.' Not impressed, I gather. 'And you, Dimitri?'

'I have plan to be professional dominant person.'

'You've come here looking for work?' She is taken aback. 'Well, we do have some members who work on the scene. I'm sure you'd benefit from meeting them. It's funny, but you really don't look or dress like the stereotype. I like that though.'

'I have no leather pants,' says Dimitri regretfully. 'Too expensive. But I have other job too. I work in Russia as an actor. I want to improve my English, get into the movies, you know.'

Mal and O are obviously transfixed by this odd foreign fish. I must admit, I'm pretty hooked myself. Is he approaching this 'dom' thing as method-acting practice, or is it a genuine predilection? I rather hope I will get to find out.

'How long have you two been playing together?' asks Mal suddenly, and I dry up. We are going to be found out and kicked down the stairs by his rather sexy steel-capped boots. Or O's gorgeous pointy stilettos. Either way.

But Dimitri saves the ball, apparently having presence of mind among his other skills. 'Not long. Maybe six weeks,' he says. 'We are learning. She don't have kinky lover before, but I do. Lots of kinky lovers for me.'

'What a wonderful time you will have here,' says O with a rather flirtatious smile. She fancies him! 'I think you're going to be valuable additions to our merry little band.'

'And now,' says Mal, leaning back to perch on his vast desk, 'for your initiation. What do you want to show us?'

Dimitri looks down at me, awaiting my pleasure.

'Um.' I can't hedge, I have to look confident, as if this is something I do all the time. 'Maybe just a little spanking.'

'Just a little one?' He curls his lip and winks at me. I have to catch my breath. 'OK.' He takes off his battered leather jacket to reveal heavily tattooed arms. I try not to look too surprised at the colourful display but it's hard not to stare.

'Gorgeous work,' purrs O. 'I presume you had these done in Russia?'

'Uh-huh,' he says, throwing the jacket into the corner of the room with a fluid motion of his sinewy arm. 'Can I get a chair, please?'

Mal obliges, pushing a plain wooden chair into the centre of the room.

'Do you need any implements?' he asks politely, then, registering Dimitri's frown, he explains, 'Straps, whips, you know.'

I put my hand on Dimitri's forearm and grip it fearfully.

'Oh, uh-huh. Well, maybe tonight Rosie is a little shy so I just use my hand, right? That's OK?'

'That's fine,' says O. 'I love the intimacy of an old-fashioned hand spanking.'

Intimacy. I look down at what I'm wearing. A thick tweedy skirt for the autumn weather, diamond-patterned opaque tights over cotton boy shorts. Kinky it ain't, unless you hanker after that librarian look. Will I have to … bare anything?

I can leave. I can just walk away. No consequences, no risks. I know what this place is now; my curiosity is sated.

Except it isn't. In its place are a dozen new curiosities about Dimitri, about S&M, about how it could feel, how it could be to have fantasies made flesh.

I watch him take his place on the chair, then he sweeps his hand in a broad gesture that starts out pointing at me and ends up slapping his thigh.

It's unequivocal enough, and so terribly sexy my cotton boy shorts flood. I shuffle over and stand by his knees, wondering if there's a graceful way to put myself across them.

His face is set and intense. He takes my arm and manoeuvres me down until my stomach presses against his strong thighs and my view is of the floor. I'm going to have to keep my eyes shut for this, I think, though I'd love to see what we look like from a third person's perspective. Perhaps Mal or O will take a photograph.

'OK, OK,' he mutters, quite gently, positioning my legs so that they are straight, tiptoes touching the floor, then he elevates his thighs a little, having an unmistakable knock-on effect on my bottom, and rubs my spine.

'This is comfortable for you?' he whispers and I nod. Actually, it really is. It feels so safe and held – it's almost as if I've come to him for protection rather than punishment.

The word 'punishment' starts my juices flowing again. My heart thunders. I'm really doing this, really putting myself across a strange man's lap to get spanked in front of witnesses. My breath hitches.

He puts his hand on my thigh, just below my skirt hem, and traces the diamond pattern with an idle finger.

'You know, Rosie, I can't have this skirt this way. It's too thick. I push it up, right?'

Oh God. I'm quivering so much from the way his finger strokes the back of my thighs that I can't speak. I just lie there while he pushes the heavy tweed up and up, over the curve of my bum, taking it unbearably slowly until I feel his palm flat on my buttocks, protected only by tights and knickers now.

'And these things,' he says, moving his palm in a circular motion over the target area while I try really, really hard not to buck and press my groin into his leg. 'What you call them? Hoses?'

'Tights,' I gasp with a giggle.

'Too tights,' he quips, and before my brain catches up with his fingers I am feeling cool air on bare flesh.

The boy shorts are cut high and a good portion of my bottom swells out from beneath their edges – more, really, than they cover. I kick out in panic, but it's hard to kick when your knees are hobbled by tights and Dimitri places a cautionary hand on the scoops of flesh he has just exposed. My rebellious nerves are quelled at once by the caress of his warm palm, moulding itself to my natural curves. It feels ridiculously good.

'OK, Rosie?' he whispers, leaning down so that only I can hear him for a moment.

'I didn't know you were going to do that.'

'No, me either. It seems right.'

'Don't take my knickers down or I'll kill you.'

'OK. Not tonight.'

He unwinds his spine and I feel him tensing, preparing. I picture him putting his shoulders back, flexing his muscular forearms. Speaking of muscular forearms, how hard is this going to be? How much is it going to hurt?

A flash of fear plunges to my stomach as I hear him – courtesy of his multitude of bangly things – raise his hand.

'You have anything to say to me before I start?'

His voice has changed. It's gruff and menacing. My insides coil, my clit fattens.

'I'm sorry,' I say. What the hell I'm sorry for, I don't know. I've been transported to another headspace.

'Who you are apologise to? To me?'

'Uh, yeah.' I catch my breath, realising what he means. 'Oh, sorry, *sir.*'

'You must learn,' he says. 'This is not respectful. I teach you respectful.'

I teach you English grammar. What would happen if I said it? I daren't imagine.

The speculation flies from my mind at the first sharp contact of his hand with my arse. It's loud and shocking and I actually laugh, as if I can't distinguish slap from tickle.

'What?' He pantomimes horror. 'You are laughing at me? I don't stand it. She is nervous.' This last presumably addressed to our audience, who chuckle understandingly. 'I get serious.'

His hand falls again, hard enough to sting, not so hard as to really hurt. I get the sense that he is holding a lot back, but what he gives is plenty. The surreality of the situation masks some of the pain – a big part of my head is engaged in establishing the fact that this is happening at all, and then trying to work out whether it's good or bad. I'm slightly detached from it, trying to capture each sensation individually rather than letting the experience take me over.

The sound of it is so satisfying, and the pain is little more than discomfort. I focus on the humiliation of my position. That's the element I want to sink into, to inhabit and explore from every angle. That's what's going to get me off tonight, after all this is done and I'm back in my bed. Think of where I am, think of what's happening to me. It's happening to me! It can't be real. Yes, it's real, I thought we'd established that.

These thoughts in a loop prevent me from getting into the mindset I thought I'd be in if and when I ever got spanked by an attractive man. I need to switch off and, as if he knows this, Dimitri suddenly ups the ante, smacking harder, lower, on the vulnerable area around the tops of my thighs, and all my thoughts are instantly diverted to the corridor marked 'Ouch'.

No room for over thinking now. Perhaps this is the antidote I have always needed. I begin to squirm and jolt. I reach back and claw at his leg, my tiny fake squeals graduating into proper yelps.

'You know I am serious,' he growls, lighting up the crease underneath the curve of my arse. 'I will make you to obey me.'

'I will, sir,' I moan, kicking pathetically. How long is this going to go on for? I curl my fingers up in the rough denim of his jeans and cling.

He speeds up and my yelps turn into a continuous keen, the peppery sting becomes a burn, searing itself tissue deep. I can't take much more – except I probably could, if I knew how many more, how much longer. It's the uncertainty, the unpredictability that is distressing me.

'Please, sir,' I cry, and he holds fire.

'Yes?'

'Are you nearly finished?'

'Are you nearly sorry?'

'Yes, sir. Very, very nearly sorry.'

'OK. Then I am nearly finished.'

I trust him, a realisation that knocks me for six. The man is a complete stranger who has somehow lured me into a fetish club so he can perform humiliating acts on me in front of other strangers, but I trust him. Either I'm profoundly stupid or I'm on to something with this guy.

My fingers unclench and I drop my legs again. I offer my heated arse to him to treat as he sees fit. I know he won't give more than I can take. I am safe with him.

My instincts prove correct. He finishes with a volley of sweet, light slaps, the stinging icing on the burning cake, then he rests one hand on the sore area and rubs my back with the other.

'You learn your lesson, right?' he says.

'Yes, sir.'

'OK. You can get up.'

I can't face Mal and O, and I turn away from them as soon as I am up, hiking up the tights and wrenching down the skirt with immoderate haste.

'Nicely done,' says Mal. 'She needs a bit of practice. She's a bit skittish.'

'Inexperienced,' says O, and there's a weight of worldly knowledge in her tone. 'She just needs to be brought on a bit. You seem well capable of the task. Anyway, welcome to Kinky Cupcake. We're very happy to have you.'

Dimitri rises from his chair and I watch him, from the corner of my eye, stride over to Mal and shake his hand with too much vigour for a man who has been using that arm to whack my behind for the last five minutes.

'Take a look around the place,' says Mal. 'You'll get a lot out of being a member, I'm sure. Anything you want to know, any ideas you have for making tweaks or improvements – we're always here. Just pop into the office. Cheers.'

'Rosie.' Dimitri's voice is no less stern than it was while I was over his knee. I almost jump to attention, wheeling around to face him with my eyes wide. 'This is good manners? Say thank you to our hosts.'

I mutter thank yous without catching their eyes and follow Dimitri back out to the landing as fast as my feet will shuffle.

He takes my hand and leads me through another door, into a capacious space that could very easily be mistaken for a regular café or bar. Blond wood floor, high spot lit ceilings, a long maple counter with large glass domes housing pretty pyramids of cupcakes and Jenga-structures of flapjacks – it's like a giant branch of Prêt.

There are differences, of course. Prêt wouldn't have quite the same prints on the walls, for instance, nor would the clientele be quite so skewed towards the rubber clad. All the same, I feel my headspace veer from submissive to 'normal' again as I breathe in the aroma of coffee.

'I'll get us a coffee,' I tell Dimitri. 'Do you want a cupcake? Do you suppose the cupcakes are actually kinky?' Reaching the counter, I frown down at the frosting of the cakes in the nearest display case. Black and red liquorice whips decorate it, formed into a very elaborate flogger design. 'Wow, that's so cool. They are.'

The handsome barista in a black silk shirt, leather pants and Zorro mask completes our order with a flourish and we take ourselves to a cream sofa in the corner, from which all things are visible.

'This is nice,' I say vaguely, sipping at my coffee and watching gorgeous exotically dressed people flit to and fro.

'You can sit OK?' Dimitri puts a hand on my spine, fingers crawling down towards my coccyx.

I flush with recollection, not wanting to talk about it. 'Fine. This sofa's very soft.'

'I don't hurt you too much?'

'No, no. It's cool.'

'Cool?' He tilts my chin up with a lone finger and makes my head swivel to face him. I drop my eyes, but he tuts and I lift them again. 'What's that? Cool? But did you like it?'

31

'Like it?'

He tips his head to one side, watching me intently. He will have his answer. Hedging is going to be futile, I can tell.

'It was … different.'

'No, Rosie. You liked it. I could tell.'

'How?'

He drops his neck low and sniffs with a dramatic flourish.

I raise a hand as if to slap him, but he catches my wrist and lowers it, chuckling. 'What? It's true. This is your thing, this spanking. This submission. Why pretend not?'

'I don't even know you.'

'You know what you need to know.'

'And what's that?'

'I like spanking and you like to be spanked. What else you need to know but that?' His grin, almost broader than his face, gleams in my eye line.

Put like that, it does sound beautifully simple. Two halves that click into a piece. It really can't be that simple, though, can it?

'Ha, well, there you go,' I say lamely, once my cheeks have reached the critical mass of blush. 'So you like this place? You think you'll, uh, come here often?'

His laugh is dirty. 'Yeah. I will come here very often. And I hope you will too. Drink that, we'll look around.'

32

He picks up a card from the sheaf tucked inside the menu.

'This week,' he reads in portentous tones, 'at Kinky Cupcake. Second of October – that's today, right? – in the dungeon at eleven p.m. – How to Use the St Andrew's Cross. In the schoolroom at eight p.m. – Lessons With Mr Strict. Hey, that was what we saw, you think? In the boudoir at midnight – Share a Slave.' He puts the card down, raising his eyebrows at me.

'It sounds like a kind of college of kink,' I muse. 'Lessons and activities. If I'd known all this was here, perhaps I'd have tried to get in sooner.'

'You think is allowed to watch any of this? Or only to join in?'

'I don't know. I feel I'd like to take a look, but I don't think I'm ready to, er, throw myself into the fray quite yet.'

'We find out.' He puts down the coffee cup, wipes his moustache with the back of his hand and pulls me to my feet.

Almost immediately, every eye in the room is upon him. Even in a place jam-packed with people in chains and gimp masks, Dimitri manages to look picturesque and striking. I feel obscurely flattered that this charismatic man has somehow latched on to me and I follow him past the counter and towards the spiral staircase beyond.

We can go up it or down it. My guess is that the dungeon

will be downstairs, along with that schoolroom we so fatefully peeked into, so we head for the basement.

A dark corridor lit with old-fashioned sconces is our destination. Three arched doors are set in the wall at intervals.

Dimitri pushes the first, gently enough, and it swings open to reveal the schoolroom, empty now. He leads me inside and we tiptoe around, running our fingertips over the desks, gathering chalk dust as we go.

'You like this?' asks Dimitri, opening the cupboard and taking out a cane, which he swishes terrifyingly.

'Christ, watch yourself with that. You'll take someone's eye out.'

'I never use one of these,' he said, flexing it into an inverted U shape. 'This could be very painful, I think.'

'Yeah, so do I. Don't even go there. I'm not ready for it.'

'One day, maybe.'

'Maybe.'

'Go on, bend over for me. I just tap you, I promise.'

'Dimitri!'

'I promise. Bend over chair, like the lady we see, I forgot her name.'

'Twinkletits or whatever it was, you mean?'

'Do it. I give you, what they say, six of the best? Except it's not the best. Six of the lightest, not painful, not at all.'

He wheedles so attractively that I can't deny him. With a sigh, I place my hands palms down on the seat of the chair and wiggle my still rather heated behind inside its skirt.

He holds the cane at arm's length and places it, very gently, across my posterior. Even the feel of it there, doing nothing, is scary. In rest, it is no more than dormant, lying in wait for the moment when it will deliver the fiercest sting in the spanker's armoury. I clench my buttocks and Dimitri taps them.

'Easy,' he says, then he brings it down, lightly as anything, on the seat of my skirt.

Any force it might have had is muffled by the thick tweedy material, but I'm far from impervious to its effect. A pleasurable shock travels through my legs, reawakening the sensations aroused by the earlier spanking.

'That hurts?' My wriggle and gasp might have given the wrong impression.

'No, it doesn't. Look, let's go and see what's next door.'

If he carries this on, I'm going to need relief.

'Oh, you don't like it.' He sounds so disappointed. 'If I hit harder?'

'Another time.' I straighten up, put a hand on his chest. 'Another time would be better. I'm worried someone will walk in and we'll get into trouble and get thrown out. And, since we've only just got here, that would be a shame.'

'Yes, it's true.' He puts the cane back on the rack with its brothers and runs curious fingers over the ranks of straps and tawses and paddles that fill the shelves.

The second room is also empty, but it's interestingly fitted out with medical trappings – various trolleys with straps hanging off them are lined up against the far wall. I spy something that looks like an enema kit, tug at Dimitri's wrist and get him out of there. That's a doctor and patient scenario too far for me right now.

The door of the third room is a little ajar, and we enter to find ourselves at the back of a small crowd, standing in the gloom watching something taking place on a stage beneath the blacked-out window.

A girl is getting her arms and legs strapped to a wooden X-shape inside a large wheel. She is completely naked, her pierced nipples standing hard and red, similar silverware glinting from her labia. She is blindfolded and, once the shirtless man by her side finishes binding her, he fits a gag around her mouth as well.

'Of course, it's up to you whether you use a blindfold and/or gag,' the man says to the audience. 'Some might see it as gilding the lily. For others, it's an essential part of the experience. Kiki here didn't start using them until she'd really got to know the cross and the way I like to play with it. As ever, trust is the watchword.'

'You've got her facing outwards,' comments a woman in the front row. 'I thought it was used more as a whipping post.'

'Aha, I want to show you some of the different uses it can be put to before we get to the classics,' says the … I guess he's one of these doms, with a smile. 'Kiki is facing out so I can be a little bit creative with those parts of her that are exposed.'

He picks up a flogger, a cute thing with a crystal handle and purple strands, and begins swishing it gently over Kiki's nipples.

The woman's teeth gnash over the gag. Her stomach undulates. I can see, even from here, her clit swell between her spread lips.

'This is the perfect opportunity to tease.' The dom chuckles. The flogger caresses Kiki's belly and thighs.

I clamp mine together, feeling a little hot and bothered, hoping Dimitri is too transfixed by the demonstration to notice.

The dom flicks the flogger between Kiki's legs, catching that sensitive inner-thigh skin, making me wince in sympathy. Tiny muffled mewls pour from her. A lacing of red patterns the whiteness on display. It must feel hot down there.

Then he begins to flick the tips upwards.

'Oh God,' I whisper, unable to help myself. How would a flogger feel just there, right on the clit, right on the cunt? Would it burn?

Dimitri puts a hand on the small of my back, as if sensing that I need steadying.

Her moans stream from her while her head rotates ceaselessly on her neck.

'A good heated cunt, just the way we like it, eh, Kiki,' drawls the dom. 'Ready to take what's coming.'

I forget how to breathe. Is there going to be live sex? If there is, will I be able to tear myself away? Dimitri's fingers are drifting up and down the hollow of my back, rather hypnotically. I'm not sure he realises he's doing it, but it's turning me on even more.

The dom puts down the flogger and reaches into the girl's shaven private parts. He rubs her clit between finger and thumb, then spears two fingers up behind. When he draws them out, he shows them solemnly to the front row.

'Wet enough, I think you'll agree. Pussy whipping is a subject for another class – don't forget to sign up for next week's session if you're interested.'

With his juiced-up fingers, he spends an idle moment or two twiddling Kiki's nipples while she strains piteously against her bonds.

'Now, Kiki, you've gone and disgraced yourself in front of our audience again, getting horny when you're meant to be informing and educating. Tut-tut. I guess that means I'll have to whip you. Now, I'm going to untie you, then you turn around so I can fasten you again, OK?'

She can hardly argue with him, mouth stuffed with silicone, but she seems happy to comply, turning obediently when her buckles are undone.

As the dom fiddles with straps, I hazard a shy glance up at Dimitri, whose eyes have darkened in fascination. His hand appears to have come to rest on my hip and he is closer to me, almost holding me against him, like a lover would.

He breaks his gaze and swivels it in my direction. 'What do you think?' he asks.

'What do I think? What do you mean?'

'This is interesting to you? You feel it makes you hot?'

I laugh nervously. The ambient temperature of this dungeon is rather cold, but I hadn't noticed until he mentioned it. 'It's interesting, of course. Hard not to be interested in girls strapped to crosses getting flogged. It's like an old Hammer horror movie.'

'But it don't make you hot?'

'None of your business.'

'Really? You think?'

He grimaces, as if I've mortally offended him, and his attention reverts to Kiki, whose plump rounded arse now faces us. Another stranger's bare bum in my sights – how many more can I expect to see tonight?

The whip is applied to back and bottom, covering her skin with fascinating line drawings until the lines begin to fill and she is a mass of raised welts.

She doesn't utter a single cry.

'Why is she so quiet?' I ask Dimitri.

He shrugs. 'Well training, I think. Is nice effect with the whip, I like.'

The dom steps back and drops the whip. 'Now, this particular cross,' he says, somewhat hoarsely, 'has a special extra feature.' He puts a hand on the external wheel and spins. Kiki's body performs one whole revolution. 'It spins. My colleague Ricardo and his submissive Jared are going to show you how you can utilise this to best effect – I'm not quite the expert with a bullwhip I'd like to be, so I'm handing over to him now.'

Unexpectedly, the spinning bullwhip demonstration provides an oasis of relief in my desert of squirmy arousal. It's too circus-act-like to turn me on and my clit returns to normal dimensions, breath speeding from my lungs as if released from long incarceration. All the same, it's fascinating to watch and I bite my lip on Jared's behalf, watching the welts rise across his pale flesh.

'Would you whip men as well as women?' I ask Dimitri. 'In your new career?'

'Sure, why not? An ass is an ass, right?'

'And would you offer sexual favours too?'

'No, I don't offer sex. Just domination, right? Maybe I fuck somebody with a dildo, who knows? I think this thing through later.' The succession of 'th' sounds nearly ties his tongue and he stumbles over the words, but I get their sense.

Fair enough.

We watch the show to the bittersweet end.

Jared, released from the cross, falls on to all fours and pushes his arse up for his master, but Ricardo just laughs and swats it.

'No way, baby,' he says. 'Nearly time for Share a Slave, and you're on the list, boy.'

Amid applause, he collars Jared and leads him, every inch the proud owner, out of the dungeon.

'Share a slave, huh?' Dimitri raises an eyebrow at me. 'You think we can watch?'

'Only one way to find out.'

Chapter Three

The crowd begins to turn and flow out of the dungeon, heading back up the stairs.

'Where's this boudoir then?' I wonder, but obviously there is no need to ask – they will lead us there.

Many people spill back into the café but others ascend to the upper floor, where the handsome barista presides with a clipboard in front of a door plastered in flock wallpaper and decorated with obscene cherubs.

'Sorry, guest list only,' he tells us. 'Our multi-partner events are limited to thirty ticket holders. There's another one next month, if you want to sign up.'

'Is some kind of orgy?' Dimitri asks.

'Some kind of.' The barista smiles. 'The café is still open, with a licensed bar, if you want to carry on socialising.'

'OK, thanks.'

'So that's that,' I say, once we are back in the café. 'Kinky Cupcake in a nutshell. Or a cake wrapper.'

Dimitri is busy looking at a pinboard full of business cards and leaflets offering specialist services. 'You see,' he says. 'This can work. Nearly all these are women. Dominatrix ... dominatrix ... submissive girls ... girls need a spanking ... I spank bad boys ... so far no man advertise.'

'That could be something to do with market forces,' I point out gently, then a horrible, horrible thought knocks me for six. Markets. Business. Advertising. 'Fuck!'

Dimitri turns to me. 'That is an order?'

'Tch. No, I mean, fuck! I haven't finished the air-freshener campaign. I'm going to get it right in the neck. Look, I have to go. Maybe if I do a bit of work from home ... but all the stuff is in the office – shit.'

'Hey, calm, calm.' Dimitri puts his hands over my arms, reining in some of my wilder gesticulations. 'What are you talking about?'

'I have a presentation to give tomorrow, but when I saw the light coming from here, I left work before I was ready. I have to finish this work! But the office is closed until seven now. And the presentation is at nine. I'm doomed. Haven't even got a slogan, let alone the PowerPoint.'

'You panic, don't panic. You work ...' He waves a hand in the direction of my office. 'Right?'

'Yeah. Over the road.'

'So that's that. I see.'

'What?'

He doesn't answer and I'm reduced to trotting across the café and down the stairs after him, voicing questions to the air around me. 'What do you mean, get me in there?'

It's chilly on the street outside. I wrap myself in my coat and frown at Dimitri, who is standing, stroking his chin and staring at my office.

'We go round the back,' he says eventually.

'Dimitri, we are not breaking into my workplace! We just aren't. There's a security guard!'

'Oh, then it's easy. You tell him you leave something up there. You have ID?'

'Yeah. But –'

'Go, go, talk to him. He let you in.'

'But once I'm in, I have to stay in.'

'Is OK, I make distraction.'

'Dimitri! Don't get yourself arrested for fuck's sake.'

'I never get arrested.' He winks. 'Never.'

I shake my head for a moment, then I think of my account manager Giles's disbelieving narrowed eyes behind his super cool spectacle frames and I shudder. I don't want to face them tomorrow. It has to be worth a try.

Mr Security is sitting at the reception desk, feet up,

reading the *Evening Standard* while black and white CCTV footage flickers on the screens overhead.

I rap at the door and press my ID badge to the smoked glass.

He peers at me, then lumbers over. 'What's to do?' he asks through the letterbox.

'I left my house keys in the office. Just came out of the pub and realised they're in my desk drawer. Can I come in and get them?'

'I'll get them for you. Where are they?'

I clench my fists. Is there any point in telling the truth? It has to be worth a try.

'Look, I haven't finished some important work. Would it be impossible to come in and do an hour's graft at my desk? Please? It could save my life – it could certainly save my job. And we all need a job in this climate.'

The guard tightens his lips, puts his head to one side. Then, 'Ah, go on.' My heart leaps as he opens the door to me and lets me slip in. 'Just for you,' he says, with a rather unsubtle wink.

'Er, thanks. Thanks a million. I owe you one.'

'That's right, love.'

I feel vaguely creeped out as I rush to the lift, grateful when its doors slide a barrier between us. All the same, it's a bit of a triumph, and Dimitri won't need to risk his liberty or his visa after all.

So what will he do now?

Reaching my desk, it occurs to me that I don't have a number for him, or an address. What if that's that and we never meet again?

Before switching on the light, I move over to the window and look down to the street. Kinky Cupcake is in darkness, even though I know that, somewhere in its upper roof space, slaves are being shared. As for Dimitri, there is no sign of him.

I sigh, flick the switch and sit down at my desk.

Air freshener. It freshens air. Four fresh fragrances. Fresh … fragrance … air … odour … aroma … I put my forehead on the desk and try to extract some coherence from these strands, but all I can think about is how Dimitri smells and how it felt to have his arm around me.

My mind dances away from scents and into sensations. Over his lap, he could have gone further, he could have touched me … right there, but I mustn't masturbate on CCTV, mustn't do that …

I wake up with a jolt. There is a hand on my shoulder.

'Dimitri?' I whisper, turning around, but it isn't.

'Sleepyhead,' says the guard with a leer. 'Off in the land of nod, were you, love?' His fingers press into my shoulder blade. I try to shrug them off, but they are planted there.

'Didn't realise,' I mumble. My head is still thick, but

my heart recognises danger, quickening into a pounding rhythm. Sweat prickles on my palms.

'I've gone out of my way for you,' he says. 'Could get into trouble for this. So that one you owe me …'

He bends lower and buries his nose in my hair. My scalp crawls as if beset with a million head lice.

'What?' I try to get the words out but my voice is high and cracked. 'This'll be on CCTV. Don't.'

His meaty hands move down my shoulders over my upper arms. 'Switched it off, of course. You think I'm stupid?' His pig's snout snuffles my neck.

I want to scream, but there's no point. The clock says five ten. Nobody will be anywhere near this place.

All I can do is moan, 'Noooo,' while he chuckles, and then an alarm shrills out, so loud and piercing that we both jump and the top of my head bangs into his chin so that he swears.

'What the fuck?' he bellows, racing over to the lift.

I stand up, sit down, stand up again, grab my bag with a shaky hand, look out of the window and around the room. He's downstairs and I don't want to encounter him again. Can I get out on the fire escape?

Headless-chicken-style, I run around the third floor, somehow unable to remember its layout even though I've been working here six months.

The shrieking in my ears doesn't help. I put my hands over them and head for the emergency exit. Somewhere before the barred door, a pair of hands grabs hold of me and I scream and flail, aiming a sharp kick for my assailant's shins.

'Rosie! It's me.'

I quit struggling and stare into the face of Dimitri.

'Was that you?' I yell over the wail of the sirens. 'The alarm?'

'Yes, I set it off.'

'What's happening?'

The alarm ceases abruptly and my ears ring with gratitude.

'Come on, I have to talk to your guard.'

'No, leave it!'

'No, come on.'

The guard is behind the reception desk, frowning and fiddling with his CCTV screens. He jumps up when he sees us. 'Oi! What's going on? I've got the police coming.'

'Better not,' says Dimitri, holding up a reel of tape. 'I've got film of you with my friend here. Bad evidence, right?'

The guard swipes for it, but Dimitri holds it up high.

'She want to tell the police you try to touch her.'

'I didn't!'

'I saw it. I have the film.'

'Look, I don't know what your game is but –'

'But when the police come, you send them away, and then you go home, right? We look after the place until it open.'

'I'll lose my job.'

'You'll lose more than your job if you don't do as he says,' I snap, taking my cue from Dimitri. Something about him makes me feel brave and invincible. 'Just do it or I'll take you to court.'

The guard looks at the tape in Dimitri's hand, looks at the CCTV, then looks back again. 'You won't say nothing about this then?'

'If you go home. And stay away from my girl. Right away.'

'OK then.'

The guard picks up the phone and makes a short call, explaining that the police are no longer needed, then he takes his rucksack and edges past us.

'Oh, one other thing,' says Dimitri politely.

The guard stops.

Dimitri slaps him hard so that the guard's chops wobble and his eyes bulge in astonishment.

'Bye bye.' He pushes the guard onwards by the shoulder. 'Don't see you later.'

'So.' I draw a breath. 'Right. That was lucky.'

'Lucky. I am lucky person.'

'You've been hanging around outside for five hours?'

'No. I go back to my friend's place. I go to sleep. But I wake up in two hours, I realise I have question for you. So I come here, see if you are still at the office. Through the window, I see this creep on the TV screen. I break in, set off alarm. Here we are.'

'Here we are.'

'You get me a coffee? In your office?'

'Oh. Sure.'

On the way up the stairs, various things Dimitri has said slot into my thought queue, once the intense relief at not having had to murder the security guard has abated a little.

'You told him I was your girl,' I mention, plugging in the coffee machine.

'What you say?'

'The security guy. You said, "Stay away from my girl."' My efforts to replicate Dimitri's accent are only partially successful.

'You want him to try again?'

'Do you think he would?'

'Not now. Not if he thinks I am your boyfriend. He fears me.' Dimitri says this with a casual air, as if it's perfectly normal for thugs of brick shithouse build to cower before him.

'I see. Well, thanks. Actually, yeah, thanks for all of that. I should have said that before. Head's not quite straight yet. Not that I needed saving or anything. I could quite easily have whacked him in the groin with my paperweight.'

Except that wouldn't have occurred to me, in my creeping panic.

Dimitri humphs and scoops coffee into the filter, not dignifying my pathetic bravado with an answer.

'That's going to be quite strong.'

'Uh-huh. Strong coffee. What we need, right?'

'What's the question?'

'Question?'

'You said you came back here to ask me a question.'

He turns and leans on the counter, primping his moustache so that the ends are perfectly symmetrical. 'If I want to be professional dom, I need to practise,' he says.

'Oh, that.' I still think he's barking up the wrong tree. Surely there aren't that many people who would pay for a bloke to abuse them?

'I will like to practise with you,' he says.

I bite my lip and watch the first few drips of coffee fall into the jug. 'Practise ... When you say practise, you mean ...?'

'You submit to me, right? I do all that whips and bondage on you. Maybe other activity too, is up to you.'

'I thought you said you'd had all these kinky girl-friends. Didn't you learn anything from them?'

'Ah, I say that for benefit of that vampire man. I never have a kinky girlfriend.'

'Oh.'

'So, you are interested? If not, is fine, I can ask the Trixietots.'

'No, no, no. No need. No. Don't do that.'

He smiles, a kind of evilly triumphant smile. 'I knew that will work,' he says. Those piercingly keen eyes crinkle, lasering into my soul.

I clatter the coffee cups crossly. 'I'm not jealous, if that's what you're thinking.'

'Yes you are.'

'What makes you think that?'

'Come here and I show you.'

My wrists, suddenly limp, can't deal with the coffee cups any more. I glance over at him, guarded but strung taut with excitement.

'Come on,' he repeats, with a tilt of the head. 'Over here, Rosie.'

It reminds me of that blurry, swoony moment before he spanked me. My pussy reacts accordingly. The command in his voice lures me to him; as soon as I am within reach, he places me between his feet and laces his fingers together around my waist.

'I think you are attracted to me,' he says in a low-down whisper that tickles my ear and, correspondingly, my crotch. 'You know why?'

'Go on.' I try to keep a sardonic edge in my tone, but the tremble betrays me. 'Enlighten me.'

'Because a girl who lets a man do this ...' He unlaces his fingers and pats my bottom, gently, but providing such a potent reminder of what happened earlier that my knees buckle. He pulls me in tighter, keeping me upright in arms that imprison as well as support. 'Really wants him to do this.'

His moustache prickles my upper lip and our noses rub together. He is giving me plenty of time to say no, plenty of time to duck back or sideswipe. I'm not doing any of it.

'Do what?' I whisper.

His answer heats my lips. 'This.'

And we kiss. I put my hands in his hair, his bushy thick mane of dark-brown hair and sink my fingers into the richness. His mouth is hot and soft at first, then more demanding, his tongue forging through to tangle with mine. When his hand slips up inside my top, I feel the cold metal of his bangles chill my skin and I wriggle a little against him, causing him to hold me firmly with a hand on my back until I am still and his travels continue. The fabric of my top rises with each new incursion until it bunches just beneath my bra and both of Dimitri's hands are planted on the exposed portion of my back.

He gives my lower lip a tiny nip and breaks the kiss.

'We can lose this,' he says, shoving the top up, over my breasts and up my arms, which I raise without question.

He kisses my mouth once more, fulsomely, then lowers his head so that his lips graze the side of my neck, turning it to gooseflesh. His palms rise to cup my breasts in the accursedly boring workday bra I am wearing. He moans onto my neck, a low keen of lust, and flicks his tongue out to wet my skin. My nipples struggle against the stout cotton, pushing themselves out for his fingers' attention, which is readily given. I rub my nose under his ear and give the ear lobe teasing bites. He moans even more, his voice vibrating down through my tissues, all the way to my bursting clit.

He smells and tastes and feels so good, it's an intoxication, a need that addles my brain and befuddles my senses. I rub my legs against his, letting my shoe drag up and down his ripped jeans, the leather making contact with patches of his skin.

He captures me in a kiss again, yanking aside the cups of my bra with one hand while the other moves lower, finding my skirt zipper and fiddling with it.

I shiver all over when his palm caresses my bare nipple, brushing it into a tight hard knot of need so that it's ready for him to pinch, very gently, exquisitely, but no less cruelly. I gasp into his mouth and a shot of sweet pain makes me grind myself against him, finding a swelling beneath those jeans that I feel more than ready to tackle.

I move my hands down to cup his behind, noticing how tightly the muscles are bunched, poised and ready for action. This butt means business. And so do this tongue, these fingers and this rock-hard jean-clad cock.

One arm reaches behind me and undoes the zipper of my skirt. As we kiss and wrestle and grind and pant, the garment makes a slow rumpled journey down over my hips, sometimes helped on its way by a free hand, sometimes left to its own devices until it reaches the point, around mid-thigh, of self-propulsion. The lining swishes past my nylon tights with a whispery crackle until it settles around my ankles. The area it once covered is now firmly annexed by squeezing, rubbing hands. I lift one leg and clamp the knee against his hip, opening myself, issuing the invitation.

Now there is nothing on my mind but visceral want. Every other consciousness has faded. I have to join my body with this one at all costs.

Whoever invented tights didn't have sex on the brain, unlike me. They stand between me and my goal in the most irritating way – there is no way of removing them without having to deal with my knee boots first. I hang on to Dimitri with one hand and try to unzip the boots with the other, keeling awkwardly to one side so that I can't maintain our kiss.

Dimitri pats me on the bottom, forcing me to look back up. 'You want to fuck?' he whispers.

Does he need to ask?

'Well, don't you?'

'I plan a kiss only. But a fuck, I don't say no, of course. Just … this is your office, yes?'

I squint at the clock. 'Yeah, but it's early. And you took out the CCTV tape for this part of the building, so … um. But perhaps you're right. Perhaps we shouldn't.'

The inopportune pause for breath has acted like a bucket of cold water. Suddenly, I'm besieged with unwelcome thoughts in the 'will you still love me tomorrow?' vein. Perhaps I'm just imagining this bond that our shared evening of randomness and debauchery has forged. He'll take what he wants and then leave.

'Wait. You don't want to?'

'I … don't know.'

'You don't know? Of course you do. Your body knows.'

'My body wants to. My brain … the jury's out.'

'OK. Well, perhaps I don't want to. Perhaps you don't respect me afterwards.'

He folds his arms and lifts his nose with offended hauteur. 'Perhaps you just use me for sex and send me away,' he says.

'I wouldn't do that.'

'No, me neither. Not to you. I have plans for you.' He fixes me with his true blue eye. 'So, sex. Yes?'

I nod. The cold water evaporates. The boots come off, then the tights and boy shorts, then I am sitting on a filing cabinet with my thighs splayed and my ankles wrapped around Dimitri's waist.

'Good. But there is a problem. I don't have no condom.'

'There are machines,' I gasp. 'In the toilets.'

56

'I run out of my pounds. They take roubles?'

'Oh God, haven't you heard of bureaux de change?' Frustrated beyond measure, I dig my heels into Dimitri's hips and then push him away, pointing at my handbag on the desk. 'Go get 'em. And be quick.'

'Yes, ma'am.' He mock salutes and races to the gents' with my handbag, looking so like the world's least convincing transvestite that I can't help giggling.

I look down at myself, naked apart from a ruined bra, sitting on a filing cabinet. The metal is cold against my backside, but I'm heating it up quickly enough. I reach around and unhook my bra. It seems pointless to keep it on, after all.

When he emerges from the toilets, condom packet in hand, I become conscious of the fact that he is still fully dressed whilst I am starkers. The inequality of the situation needs to be redressed, I feel. Or undressed.

He slings my handbag back on the desk with a pleasingly cowboy-like nonchalance and stands in front of me, hand on hip, condom brandished, crooked smile in full effect under that moustache.

'So,' he says.

'So, you're wearing too many clothes. And I'm getting cold up here.'

'Cold? Oh, that's not good.' He shimmies back up to me, clasping his hands together in the small of my back, leaning his forehead against mine. 'I don't like cold.'

Behind me, I can feel his hands waggling about, tackling the condom wrapper. It's not going to do much good unless those jeans come down, though, so I reach towards his belt buckle. Except there's a problem here – he has more than one. He is wearing about five skinny leather belts of different designs, all interlinked and looped around each other. I sigh, lips brushing his.

'Why so many belts?'

'I don't want to pack them.'

'Oh right.' One down, the other four are quick enough to unbuckle. They fall aside like a gateway of tooled leather, allowing me to concentrate on unbuttoning his fly. Here it comes. The exertion causes me to pant slightly, my hot breath mingling with his. I prepare myself to push down the jeans then the underpants – but there are no underpants. An unexpected cock emerges from the disintegrating denim, causing me to squeal inelegantly.

'You bad, bad man!' I exclaim with a delighted laugh. 'No pants!'

'OK, you got me,' he said softly. 'When I come here, I have plan to fuck you. I think maybe I can be lucky so I don't put on them.'

'You didn't think about the condoms though?' I put a hand on his cock, running my fingertips gently up the shaft, admiring its firmness.

'I don't want to be too hopeful. In Russia we believe in fate.'

His hands unclasp and he brings the unwrapped condom around, removing my fingers so he can skin it on.

'So, I am ready,' he whispers. 'You are ready?' He answers his own question by fingering my pussy, gathering my wetness as evidence.

'I'm ready.'

'I know.' He pulls my thighs apart and around his waist again, takes his cock in hand and guides it to my willing slit, rubbing it around in my juices before surging forward.

I cry out and hang on for dear life around his neck, adjusting to the strange fullness, something I have not felt for some time.

He keeps one arm anchored around my waist while he uses his other hand to stroke my clit, holding himself heroically still for a moment.

He kisses me. 'Feels good?' he asks.

'Oh. You don't need to ask. Yes.'

'OK. Hold tight.'

I cling like a spider monkey while he shunts back and forth, building up speed. The cabinet rattles underneath me, then it begins to rock, but I couldn't care less, every part of me focused on the friction inside me. He angles himself perfectly and crosses my sweetest spot, keeping the pressure on my clit at the same time. In a fog of exquisite, tormenting sensation I feel the burn at the pit of my stomach that signals the first steps on the stairway to orgasm.

'Oh, yes, hard, do it hard,' I mutter in delirium, wanting to spur him to his own. He slams the cabinet into the wall, thrusting like a madman, holding me in a tense armlock. My end is near, the sensation rising and spreading. I bury my face in his neck and start to whimper.

He says something totally unintelligible but wildly sexy-sounding – presumably in Russian – and that's what finally gets me there, bucking and writhing against him while he utters god-knows-what into my ear.

God-knows-what gets louder and more emphatic, almost vengeful in tone, until it breaks down into a formless roar and he makes his final blinding thrusts before holding himself still inside, head thrown back, beautiful throat exposed, hands gripping me to the point of bruising.

Christ. He's completely taken me. One night, one fuck, and I'm in love.

This wasn't part of the plan.

Help.

Chapter Four

I still have no idea how I made it through the day without getting fired.

I bluffed through the campaign meeting with the rapidly extemporised slogan 'What the Nose Knows' – madly, the account manager loved it. No accounting for advertising taste, obviously. Nobody commented on the smudgy black line on the paintwork behind the filing cabinet either. A few people noticed the dark circles under my eyes, especially Anton, but I put that down to staying up all night working on the campaign.

At the coffee shop around the corner, he props me up with a large macchiato after work and quizzes me on some aspects of my story that he feels don't add up.

'So were you in the office when there was that security alert?' he asks, biting off the end of his biscotti.

'Security alert?'

'Yeah, broken window on the ground floor at the back. Apparently, the alarms were activated but the police never showed up. Nobody can get hold of Whatsisname the night watchman.'

'No, I guess I went home before that.' I yawn.

'The weirdest thing about it is the missing tape from the CCTV. Just gone, man. Mental! Conspiracy!'

'I can't really think straight, Anton. Do you mind if we just talk about really straightforward, really unchallenging stuff?'

He winks. 'Same as always then?'

My phone bleeps and I try to peer through the blur to read the message. It's from Dimitri. My heart leaps and I suppose I probably blush like a fool.

'You meet me tomorrow?' it says.

'Sure. When and where?'

'Meet me 12 mid of day outside the Kinky Cupcake.'

'OK xxx.'

I wait a moment to see if he will send me anything more, with the crucial kisses, but he doesn't, so I sigh mildly and put my phone away.

'Who was that?' Anton is frowning.

'Just a mate. From home.'

'No it isn't. Your eyes did that looking up to the

left thing that's meant to be a classic sign of a fib.'

A plague on pop psychology and body language analysis.

'Anton.' I'm surprised and a little perturbed at how much this seems to matter to him. 'It's personal. OK?'

'You've got a boyfriend,' he accuses. 'You went all misty and pink. You're in love. Who is he? Not Dale from upstairs or I'll puke.'

'Jesus, no! Look, I'm too tired for this. I'm going. Thanks for the coffee. Have a good weekend.'

I sail off with my handbag clutched to my chest before he can argue.

* * *

The next day is rainy so I hurry along the Shoreditch alleyways with my umbrella and raincoat. Only I know that underneath the waterproof veneer, I am wearing only a swishy jersey dress and stockings. If going commando is good enough for Dimitri …

To my relief and near-surprise – because I was starting to wonder if I'd dreamed him – he stands in the archway of the Kinky Cupcake door. No umbrella, fatally wounded leather jacket the only thing standing between his rangy body and the elements. His moustache drips when he kisses me an enthusiastic hello.

'This is London,' I tell him. 'It rains.'

'Oh, rain.' He shrugs vaguely. 'It's nothing. In Moscow right now is first winter snow.'

'You're a tough cookie,' I say, swooning slightly at his manly disregard of the weather.

'No.' He points one finger at the dark brick behind us. 'I am a kinky cupcake. Shall we go in?'

'OK.'

We nod to the doorman and head up to the café, which is half full of damp Saturday shoppers popping in for their quota of rubber and depravity before the football scores. Actually, a rubber outfit would be good in this weather. Maybe I should get one.

'So,' I open, bringing coffee and Danish pastries to the table, 'what are we doing here?'

'I book a room,' says Dimitri, teeth flashing as he smiles his wicked smile.

'You booked a room? Here?'

'Yeah. I need to practise my skills for my new career.'

'Oh, that.' I bite my lip. I still can't quite believe he means to go through with it. 'Is it expensive? To rent the room?'

'I pay for an hour. Is quite expensive, but yesterday I find a job for while I wait for good-paying clients.'

'Good idea. What's the job?'

'In a kitchen.' He shrugs. 'It isn't for ever.'

'I'm sure.'

'So drink your coffee. I book the room one till two.'

'Which room did you book?'

'The schoolroom.'

'I see. And what might we be practising?'

'I am going to whip you,' he says, infinitely casual, dabbing coffee from his moustache with a napkin.

'Lovely.' I shudder and have the urge to hug myself. I have this sense of being in exquisite danger. Danger I have signed up for.

I linger over the coffee, keeping an eye on the clock, while we discuss my advertising campaign, his associates in the squatty-sounding dive he is staying in, his new kitchen-portering job, until the time comes and I can divert him with light chatter no longer.

He holds out his hand. 'Come.'

I hope so.

But first I have to descend with him into that sinister basement where all things dark and dreadful take place. No events are taking place this lunchtime – those are reserved for the evening hours – so the corridor is quiet. In the medical room, there seems to be a little activity going on – another booking, presumably.

Dimitri pushes open the door to the schoolroom, as white and bare and chalk-dusty as I remember with its row of little desks and its cupboard of pain.

It is to this last that Dimitri addresses himself, opening the door and pulling out a gown of coarse black material.

'This fits me?' He puts it over his shoulders and flaps about like a vampire bat, trying it out for size. It's a little short on him, but the effect transforms him from pure gypsy to, I dunno, scholar gypsy.

'You look a bit like Dracula,' I say, doubtfully. 'Maybe the mortar board?'

'The …?'

'Square hat thing.'

'This?' He perches it at a jaunty angle and tosses his head so the tassel swings.

'Why didn't my head teacher look like that?' I wonder aloud, then I squeak when he finds the cane and swishes it dramatically through the air.

After a few moments of fencing with an invisible opponent, he flexes it in both hands and fixes me with an evil grin. 'So, my naughty girl, are you ready to bend over?'

'Um. Could we start with something a little gentler?'

'Of course. Actually, I am thinking perhaps first I need to know what this things feels like.'

He rummages in the cupboard, producing a number of implements and laying them in a fan shape on the nearest desk.

'You mean, you mean, I use them on you?' I pick up a varnished wooden rectangle with a narrow handle at one end and smack it experimentally into a palm.

'Sure. If I become an expert dom, I want to know

66

what submissive is feeling. Otherwise how do I make best decision of what to do?'

'That makes a lot of sense.'

'Of course.'

Without further discussion, he whips off the cloak, turns his back to me and drops his jeans.

The sudden revelation of his tight backside causes me to cover my mouth with a hand. 'Oh,' I say, when I've caught my breath. 'Right. So, what shall I use first?'

'Your hand, maybe.'

I approach him with tentative steps and bend a little, inspecting that gorgeous arse at closer quarters.

'Yes? You can start.'

My first smack is hardly worthy of the name, pathetic really, more like a tap.

He exhales impatiently. 'What was that?'

I land a harder one. My palm tingles but his butt doesn't change colour at all.

'Did you start yet?'

Cheeky bugger. I pull back my arm and whack.

'Ah. I felt that one. Harder now.'

I look at my palm, which is an angry shade of pink just from that one stroke.

'It hurts my hand,' I object.

He sighs. 'Try the leather one.'

I pick up a short, thick strap and flap it half-heartedly.

67

'Do it hard!' he shouts, making me jump.

'Sorry,' I snipe, then I snap it down. I'm rewarded with my first flinch of the day.

'OK,' he says, putting a hand on the faint red stripe I've made. 'That is a sting. Try the wood.'

I notice that he braces himself with one hand on the teacher's desk for this one. He is expecting it to hurt. I wish I could see if it was having an arousing effect on him, but I'm at an angle to his rear that makes peeking impossible. Damn it.

I take the wooden rectangle and slap it smartly down. He hisses, but asks for a harder blow all the same.

This one makes a fierce red mark across the central part of his arse and he shakes his head vigorously while the force of the blow sinks in.

'Good,' he says. 'That is harder. Deeper pain. Now, OK, I think the cane.'

I pick up the length of rattan but I'm a little concerned. I don't know what to do with the bloody thing. What if I seriously injure him? I lay it softly across his bottom. He reaches around and pushes the tip away from his hip, further towards his arse crack.

'Don't you see how he did it that night? Was like this.'

I'm glad *somebody* was taking notes. I was too busy trying to stop myself masturbating in the street.

'A good stroke, Rosie. I want it to hurt.'

I'm scared, I can't deny it. I tap the rod, the way I think

I must have seen someone do in a film or something, and draw back my forearm, then I hear the whoosh of air as the cane rushes forwards and, just as I see Dimitri's shoulders tense, my arm freezes and I can't do it.

'Sorry, sorry, I just can't. I just can't hurt you.'

He looks over his shoulder, pensive, disappointed. 'I guess you are not a sadist,' he says. 'Not a, what was it, switch. But please, Rosie. I need to feel it. Don't think about my pain. Tell yourself this is what he wants. He wants to learn. OK? Please?'

I take a moment to recover. I see his knuckles, white from gripping the edge of the desk. He wants me to do this.

I pull back my arm again, shut my eyes for a moment and try to disconnect the act from its consequences. He is a cushion, a mannequin, something that doesn't feel pain.

I open my eyes and slice the cane through the air. Its sinister whistle makes me cringe, but I keep it moving until it makes contact with Dimitri's bottom, which quivers. His hips roll and he gasps, but there is no cry.

At first, the line I have drawn is white, then it begins to darken rapidly while Dimitri pitches back and forth on the balls of his feet. He reaches behind to touch the welt, running a fascinated fingertip along its length.

Appalled at myself, I drop the cane back on the desk. 'Oh God, that must have really hurt. I'm so sorry.'

He lets go of the desk and turns back round, hitching up his jeans with one hand while the other continues to rub his bottom.

'Well, yes, it hurt,' he confirms.

There isn't a sniff of an erection. Seems he's no switch either.

'You didn't enjoy it?'

'No, I don't like pain. Not my thing. But now I know what it feels like, so I thank you.'

'You're welcome.' I put a hand on his cheek and stroke it. 'I didn't enjoy it either. Well, maybe a little bit.' I smirk, feeling like a super-villainess in a latex catsuit.

'It's OK,' he whispers, bending to my ear. 'I am getting my revenge. It's your turn now.'

I flutter. 'Oh dear.'

'Mmm, oh dear, my dear.' His hand cups my buttocks, a menacing gesture if I ever I felt one. 'You are wearing no panties!'

'Oh. So I'm not. I knew I'd forgotten something.'

He chuckles darkly and kisses the underside of my ear. 'Bad mistake.'

I falter for a moment. 'Dimitri?'

'Umm hmm?' His fingertips bunch the skirt of my dress, rubbing it up and down my naked bottom.

'Why do you want to hurt me? Why do you like it?'

'Hey.' He draws back his neck, finding my eyes with

his. 'Because you want me to. Is no other reason. Because I want to make you hot. Turn you on, you say, no?'

'Yeah. You want to turn me on. OK. Just asking.'

I can see why people would want to be dominated, I just have some trouble getting why others want to dominate. It's hard not to question the impulse or suspect that there might be an agenda of hatred or abuse behind it sometimes.

What if it turns out that Dimitri hates women, or British people, or is just working out and passing on some horrible experiences from his past? I think that might break my heart. I know I barely know him but ...

Anyway, I believe him. There's a transparency and a zest about him that make it easy to accept that he is simply enjoying himself, and living for the moment. As to whether he wants to pleasure *me* or simply pleasure a Random Submissive Woman, the jury's out. I hope it doesn't stay out for long though.

'Good. So bend over.'

The time for angst has passed.

Dimitri takes me by the upper arm and leads me to a chair – maybe the one that Trixie Twinkle Twat was standing on that time – then places a hand on my stomach, gently pivoting me into the prescribed contortion until I am bending over, palms flat on the seat, bum up, legs hip width apart.

The hem of my dress flutters reassuringly around my

thighs, but not for long, because Dimitri's next act is to lift it up, revealing my helpless bare bottom to his disciplinary gaze.

Damn it, I'm wet already. Can he tell?

'Bad girl,' he says, grazing my inner thighs with his fingernails, almost up to the split lips of my crotch. Oh, he can tell. 'What shall I do with you?'

'I don't know,' I whisper. 'Sir.' The addition feels natural, and he seems to like it, making a low sound of approval.

'I'm going to punish you, Rosie. I'm going to use different things and see how long it takes for you to ask me to stop, OK?'

'OK, sir.'

'If you need a break, you tell me. If you can't take no more, you tell me. Right?'

'Right.'

He claps his hands together and rubs them, ready to get down to work. 'First I use this leather, OK? I start easy.'

Despite this reassurance, I clench my fists and tense up. The first contact of strap on skin is a caress, however, and I soon relax into it, enjoying each little flick of warmth as it travels slowly across the full area of my rear.

'Mmm.' I give my verdict. 'Feels nice. Really nice. Erotic.'

'Oh yes? I go harder.'

He is as good as his word, putting a little more force behind each stroke so that they sizzle rather than tickle, the heat building with each little set of snaps.

I begin to wriggle, trying hard not to break my position, then he goes harder still and the strap cracks down, lines of solid heat burning the width of my bum.

I get to twelve, I think, then I plead for a break.

He rubs my spine while I gather my breath and my wits, moving his hand lower and lower until it caresses my hot bottom.

'Looks good,' he tells me. 'You like it?'

'Yeah. It hurts but I could take more. Just needed a break. Not ready to finish yet, unless you want to.'

'OK, that is useful information. I use this for warm-up or for long erotic spanking. There is heavier thing in the cupboard, maybe that is for punishment.'

'Maybe,' I agree, distracted by the pooling of juices between my heated pussy lips. I think back to the demonstration we saw in the dungeon next door. Will Dimitri flog my pussy? I don't think I'm ready for that yet. A simple fingering will suffice today. Perhaps now?

But he isn't ready to oblige yet. My bottom must suffer on.

'Shall we start again?' He pats my recovering bum, still warm, but not particularly sore, though the skin feels tight and sensitive.

'OK, sir.'

The worst part of this is the strain on my thigh and calf muscles, I think to myself. Then I change my tune.

Wood meets flesh in a bloodcurdling duet of pain and anguish.

'OW!' I yell in objection, leaping upright and clutching my backside.

Dimitri laughs and taps the paddle on to the site of its first assault. 'That is a good one, eh? Hurts a lot?'

'Yes, it bloody does.'

'OK, I take it easier to start. Back down, please.'

I eye him suspiciously, but eventually resume my position, trusting him to do as he has promised.

He applies the paddle with a lighter hand. It still hurts, but it's bearable for twenty moderate strokes. I settle into the sensation, enjoying the uncompromising crack of the swats as they bounce and echo off the prison-white walls. Occasionally, I have to shift from foot to foot or howl out loud, until I am shifting and howling almost perpetually and then he ups the ante again, dealing six solid shockers. After the sixth I beg for mercy and he stops again.

My bottom is throbbing, the heat searing way down below the skin. Sitting down will definitely need to be done with care.

'That will bruise,' he decides, pressing fingertips into my flesh so that I wince. 'So I take it easier if client don't want bruises.'

74

'I love your … scientific approach … to this,' I pant, rational thought being far from my own mind. 'I never realised … being a laboratory assistant … could be this … interesting.'

'Ah, my assistant.' He seems to like this thought. He drops to a crouch to look more closely at the state he has made of my bum, thumbs pressed into the under hang of my cheeks. 'You know, in Russia we have a saying: Without torture, no science.'

'Really? Well, you're a great scientist then.'

He laughs and kisses my right arse cheek. I hold on to my breath while my pussy spasms. *Oh, kiss me lower, kiss away my juices.*

His lips drift down and, when he speaks, his words buzz against my nether lips. 'You don't want the cane?'

'Not today. Not ready.' I push back. He plants a lingering kiss on my wettest spot. 'Please, oh, please.'

'I lock the door.'

The most welcome words I could hear. I let my neck and shoulders relax and drop my forehead to the worn-smooth wood of the chair, then rest my cheek against its grain. My bottom still throbs, the skin stretched taut and sizzling, and my legs are starting to ache, the knees feeling locked, but I don't care. I want one thing, and I want it from him.

'This science, it make me want to fuck,' he says gravely, returning to my open legs and pushing his hand between them. 'I think for you also.' His fingers pinch and squeeze and rub. 'You are comfortable there? Your legs shake.'

Maybe a bit less pressure on my feet might be good. But there is no bed in here.

He kisses me, carefully, on the inside of each thigh, then he braces his arms around my waist and lifts me to my feet until I am held with my head in the crook of his shoulder, leaning back into him, ready to fall and be caught.

'Mm.' He kisses my neck, sucking lightly at the tender skin. 'I think here is best.'

He leads me to a gymnasium vaulting horse at the back of the room and lifts me on to it so that my stomach is cushioned by the leather-padded top and my legs dangle down, not quite reaching the floor.

I hear him shuck off his robe and unbuckle the many belts. There is a snap and the smell of latex hits my nostrils. I am ready ... set ...

And we're off.

He takes it slowly, penetrating me with care and attention to my rapidly bruising bottom.

I like the feel of him behind me, between my thighs, standing and thrusting forwards while I flounder over the horse. I feel very small and submissive, stuck here with no choice but to take my punisher's cock until he is satisfied that I have understood the nature of our bond. Him on top, giving it; me underneath, taking it.

I spread my legs wider, to give him better access, enjoying the speed and friction of his movement and the way it sends him deeper. His balls swing and bang against my sex with each homeward drive. I begin to hang on for dear life, trying to keep in position for him, trying not to slump and fall into oblivion.

Objectively, I know that my bottom must still hurt, but I don't feel it any more; I don't feel anything but the slow sensation unravelling through my groin and stomach.

His hands creep around the front of my thighs and find my clit, each set of fingers playing it like a piano while he thrusts ever harder and faster.

I come, humping my abdomen against the padded leather, digging my fingernails in until it is close to tearing. He takes hold of my hips again and gives me the final few race-to-victory lunges until he rests, embedded in me, hissing out that steaming stream of Russian phrases.

Slowly, I become aware that my bottom still hurts. Especially when he pats it and asks how I am.

'It's really sore,' I say. 'But God, that was good. So good.'

'Wait there. I see cream in the closet.'

I maintain a blissful flop over the vaulting horse while he sorts his jeans out and heads over to the cane cupboard. For a fearful second, I think he is playing a horrible trick on me and he will come back with a length of rattan, but he doesn't. Instead, he stands behind me, slathering on a cool and soothing lotion.

'Will you do that for your clients?' I ask, the words coming out slowly and heavily.

'What? This cream? If they like.'

'No, I mean sex. I think they call it "extras". In the trade.'

'I tell you before, I don't think so. I don't fuck my clients. I am not prostitute.'

'But what are you, then? You'd definitely be a sex worker.'

'Sex worker who does not have sex.'

'That's perfectly possible. All this – the headmaster stuff – is all sexual. Isn't it?'

'Yeah, but you can pretend it is not. Is different than prostitution.'

'Pretending. So it'd all be a bit of a game.'

'Sure. A bit of fun, for pay.'

'What if you wanted to have sex with a client? And they wanted it too?'

'What if, what if.' He smears on the last of the cream and recaps the tube. 'What is this?'

I sigh. 'Oh, nothing. It doesn't matter.'

'Your voice. You are not fine.'

'I am fine. Really.'

He helps me off the vaulting horse and holds me against him, his lips on my hair. 'This sex is very amazing,' he says. 'Thank you for it.'

I am instantly cheered. 'That's OK,' I say. 'You're more than welcome.'

'I wish I don't have to start work in half an hour. But I must go. I book a room for next Saturday, right?'

'Oh, yeah. Yeah. Think my bottom might have recovered by then.'

'OK. But I go for the dungeon. I think we do bondage next, yes?'

'Uh. Yeah.'

'Good. So how about we get quick cup of coffee now. Get your coat.'

Chapter Five

What with one thing and another, we didn't get the chance to meet up again until Saturday. If he was free, I was in the office. If I was free, he was in the restaurant kitchen. We had a couple of text catch-ups during the course of the week (Him: How is your ass? Me: Bruised! And so on) but didn't really speak.

I spent long days longing for him, trying to keep his image alive in my mind's eye while I wrestled with advertising copy and the many childish distractions of life in a modern media industry.

Anton worked hard to drag me away from my preoccupations. He got free tickets to a red carpet premiere in Leicester Square, then an invitation to a private view in a local gallery. Between that and my seemingly unending sloganeering, I managed not to pine too terribly.

On Friday afternoon, though, it nearly went horribly wrong.

'You fancy hanging with me and some of the crew from the baby food account tomorrow afternoon?' asked Anton in between bouts of Facebooking. 'Thinking of heading up Westfield, then whatever.'

'That'd be – oh, hang on. Sorry. Can't.'

'No? Date with Mr Mystery?'

He had been teasing me about my 'secret man' all week.

'No, just busy. Stuff to do.' I was conscious of not looking him in the eye and shuffling stuff on the desk in an evasive manner.

'Have I said something to offend you?'

'No! Of course not.'

'Westfield's a bit weak really, innit? What if I said somewhere else? Where do you want to go?'

I found the courage to look up. 'Nowhere, mate. It's cool. We'll do something on Sunday if you want.'

He brightened. 'Nice one. Brunch? Hampstead Heath?'

'Get your kite out.'

'I will! Well, I would if I had one.'

'Sorted.'

Ten minutes of silence while our heads went back down to our computer screens.

'Definitely a brothel,' he said, out of the blue, pulling me away from my air-freshener radio ad.

'What?'

'That place.' He jerked a thumb towards the window, indicating Kinky Cupcake.

'Why do you say that?'

'Just saw this blatant ho come out the door. Skirt up to her arse, heels like Nelson's Column, corset and a dog collar.'

'Perhaps that's just her style. Not very nice to call women hos, Anton.'

'Style? It's nasty. Saw a really weird guy come out of there earlier on too.'

'Did you?' I hoped to God I wasn't not blushing too much. My heart was skittering.

'Looked like one of the Village People but skinnier. I reckon they have male and female hookers in there.'

'Right. Which Village Person was it? The one with the huge feather headdress?'

'Nah. Which was the one with the huge 'tache?'

My heart stopped for a beat.

Coincidence.

Paranoia.

Stop it.

* * *

82

I want to ask him about it, but I manage to head myself off, concentrating instead on small talk about his crazy flatmates and the film I saw with Anton, while we sip at our Kinky coffee.

'I miss you this week,' he says, putting a hand on my thigh and squeezing.

'Me too.' A rush of scalding love, head to toe. 'All work and no play ...'

He doesn't know the saying.

'I play a little bit,' he says, and for a moment I think he is going to say he's been having hot kinky sex with Tinkle Tosser while I've been at work. 'We play five-a-side football, me and my friends.'

'Oh, ha ha, oh, right, oh, that's good.'

He eyes me, a little puzzled. 'You like football?'

'No.'

Over by the bar I notice a familiar-ish figure and I purse my lips.

Her, simpering between two burly blokes in suits, wearing not much more than a silk bandage and a smile. She has an amazing figure, full and womanly yet somehow lacking an ounce of extraneous flab. Her laughter is infectious and forces you to look over.

'Shall we get down to the dungeon?' I ask, trying to drink my coffee too quickly and burning my tongue.

'What is hurry? We have all afternoon.'

'Just ... can't wait.'

He chuckles, pats my thigh. 'I will make you wait. That is cruel thing to do, right?'

'Not too long though.'

She is looking over. She has clocked Dimitri. One hand primps her hair while the other slides down the curve of her hip. She thrusts out her bosom. The only way she could make it more obvious she wants Dimitri's attention is by shooting a flaming arrow across the room to him.

She catches his eye. He nods and smiles, then turns back to me.

A riot of cheering breaks out somewhere behind my ribs.

'No,' he says. 'Not too long. Is punishment for me to wait too long.' He winks and I glow. He pushes the coffee cup away and takes my hand, leads me to the Promised Land. Well, the door to the basement stairs anyway.

'Hiiiii,' says Twat Face as we pass. 'Great to see you here. Are you coming to the orgy tonight?'

'I must work,' says Dimitri, not stopping.

'Oh well. Another time. Catch you later. Unless you catch me first.' Giggle, simper.

'Later,' he says and we are through the door, away from the danger zone.

'She's very attractive,' I say, feeling my way down the dark stairs in Dimitri's wake.

'So are you,' he replies gallantly.

84

'Not in her league, though.'

'She is football player?'

'Not as pretty as her,' I translate.

'I am sad when girls talk like this. Don't say that, please.'

'It's true.'

'You say it again and I spank your ass, Rosie.'

Shivery delight. I'm tempted to say it again, but I refrain.

The door looks like a real dungeon door from some medieval castle – black metal studs, heavy oak, the works.

When I enter, it looks unfamiliar, perhaps because it was filled with people last time and now it is empty. Intimidated, I take an instinctive step towards Dimitri, who puts an arm around me.

'It looks real.' The atmosphere of pain and terror dampens my ardour for a while. I cast my eyes around the gloom, seeking adjustment.

It is lit by flaming torches. The brick, which would presumably be dark red, has been painted black. Shadows loom everywhere – exaggerated shapes of the dungeon equipment I see around me.

Oddly designed chairs and benches line the walls, most sporting leather or metal cuffs in strategic places. Set alongside these are devices resembling old-fashioned stocks or pillories, some with benches or other equipment attached. On the stage, the cross we saw in action stands like an altar, while cages and other unidentifiable constructions dot the floor space.

Dimitri plays with some of the furniture, most of which seems to be adjustable. I run my hand over a long bench with a square box at one end, the top of which looks like a toilet seat.

'What the hell's this?' I wonder aloud.

Looking over, Dimitri smirks. 'I don't think you want to know,' he says. He opens a cupboard and takes out a length of chain with leather cuffs at each end. 'So,' he says, stretching it menacingly taut before jingling it at me. 'What do you want to be tied to?'

'I'm not sure. Some of them don't look very comfortable.'

'I think this is on purpose.'

'I suppose so.'

'OK, I choose one to start. Here, this table.'

I walk over and inspect it. It's a high-set black-padded rectangle with a pair of restraining arches that would cover, approximately, the neck and the ankles. Extendable attachments at the side can be used to cuff wrists and ankles, if the arches don't suit or the legs need to be spread. It looks so cold and clinical that I want to shudder. But I'm with Dimitri. This is exploratory fun. I'm safe.

'OK,' I say dubiously. 'So ...'

'Well, of course, you must take off your clothes. You must be naked for bondage, right?'

'Oh.' I laugh, nervous and feeling the cold. 'That's right.'

He seems to tune in to my mild anxiety, stepping forwards and grabbing the lapels of my jacket. 'I help you,' he offers, sliding it off my shoulders.

The slinky top and skinny jeans test his disrobing skills, but he passes easily, stripping me down to knickers and bra with expert touch. I surrender to an urge to wrap my arms around him and bury my head in his oversized and somewhat threadbare fisherman's jumper, breathing in the reassuring scent of his rolling tobacco and joss-stick smoke and menthol. He smells outdoorsy, like a woodsman or something. Not that I've ever met a woodsman. What actually is a woodsman? It's unusual in London, anyway, where nearly everyone smells of exhaust fumes.

'You are worried?' He hugs me tight, a bone-crushing embrace just the way I like it. 'Hey, is only me. No big bad wolf.'

'You could be a big bad wolf,' I say, emerging from the sweater to look him in the eye. 'For all I know.'

'You really think?'

'I hardly know you.'

'What do you want to know? I tell you everything. We can go back to café, do this another time. Is a lot to ask, to tie up a girl when there is not time for trust –'

'But I do trust you. I'm sure I do. It's OK. You've paid for this room, we shouldn't waste your money.'

'Money.' He makes a dismissive *pshaw* type sound.

'Tie me to the table,' I say softly. 'But first, take off my underwear.'

To be honest, the feeling of being held by him wearing only bra and knickers is so sensually delicious that I can't face getting dressed again. His bear-like warmth against my nudity makes me want to snuggle up closer and closer until we are forced to merge with one another.

He unclips my bra and the sensation is enhanced by the inevitable friction of my nipples against the scratchy wool of his jumper. His mouth presses heat into mine, tongues meeting in the middle, while he works on my knicker elastic. I rub my pussy, neatly shaved for the occasion, into the crotch of his raggedy jeans. My pubis and lower abdomen encounter strips of cold studded leather, imprinting its patterns into my skin.

One of his hands reaches down to my bottom and cups it. 'How is this?' he asks, breaking the kiss.

'Oh, fine,' I whisper. 'Just a few tiny bruises left now.'

'Today, no pain,' he promises. 'Only pleasure.'

I squirm against him, wondering how the pleasure will be delivered.

'Now, on to this table.'

Not sure whether to put myself face down or up, I perch on the edge of the thing, hands clasped tightly in my lap.

He lifts the neck and ankle arches and instructs me

88

to lie down on my back, which I do. The leather is cold and clammy against my back, bottom and thighs. The narrowness of the table makes me clamp my legs together.

Dimitri lowers the neck arch, securing my head, but he removes the one lower down and places my ankles in the side-attached cuffs instead. When they are secure, but not too tight, he pulls them out, notch by notch, until my legs are well spread. This process is repeated with my wrists, so that I am a secured starfish, unable to move or raise my head. The neck arch prevents me from seeing what is actually happening lower down my body. If Dimitri moves beyond my hips, or crouches down, I can't see what he is doing to me. He could do anything. I wouldn't know until he was doing it.

My cunt spasms and I know I am wet and ready. There is nothing I can do but stare at the ceiling. At the hooks attached to beams that run beneath the ceiling. Interesting.

I hear his footsteps. He is back at that cupboard. There is much metallic rattling and some ruminative tutting.

I don't see him walk back, I just hear him. His footsteps stop somewhere near my left set of toes.

'What are you going to do to me?' I have to ask.

'Something really terrible,' he says.

A barely there ticklish sensation wisps over my toes. I wiggle them and flex my foot. The ticklishness re-sites itself to my instep and I gasp, trying in vain to yank my foot away.

'No!' I squeal. 'You can't do this!'

He appears by my head, brandishing a black marabou feather duster. 'Oh yes I can. I can do anything. You can't stop me.'

He sings the words, then glides back down, dusting me thoroughly and maddeningly, up my legs to the knees, then across my convulsing stomach, beneath my helpless armpits, over my stiffening nipples. Then over them again. And again.

He flutters those feathers so teasingly and so well that I feel my spine twist like an angry snake, working so hard and so pointlessly at removing me from the source of my aggravation.

'Oh, Dimitri, noooo.' The duster is swishing along my inner thighs. I jolt up and down, lifting my bottom from the leather, but he just darts the feathers underneath and the tickle trickles along the crack of my arse instead. I lower it abruptly, hoping to trap the damn thing, but he whips it out and reapplies it to my spread and juicy pussy lips.

'I hope that thing's clean,' I say, suddenly panicked.

'Relax, it's cool. We put all the used toys in a bag and take them to reception after. They are good with cleanness.'

'Cleanliness.'

'Yes, that. You correct me, you get extra tickle.'

I scream as he flicks the thing from side to side of my

pussy lips, rapidly and without mercy. My clit must be enormous by now; I picture it catching the feathers with its sticky juices, so they are stuck fast and can't tickle me any more.

But before that can happen, the feather duster is discarded.

'Did that feel nice?' he wants to know, but his tone is devilish.

'I hate tickling!' I pout. 'Thanks for stopping though.'

'You hate it?' I feel his fingers splay high up on my inner thigh, almost on my outer labia. 'Not so much. This is very wet here.'

'It's not.' I don't know why I feel compelled to lie. Something about being so helpless and restrained makes me want to assert myself by being contrary.

Dimitri simply laughs. 'OK, it's not. If you say so. What is next? You are wondering?'

'Of course. What is it? Is it nice?'

'You tell me.'

I hear a squirting sound, and then his fingers rubbing something into my breasts and around my nipples and …

'Oh God, that's freezing cold! Oh God! So cold it burns!' I feel my nipples contract and my whole body shiver under his touch. 'You aren't going to put it …?'

A dot of it lands on my clit, travelling by fingertip.

The icy torment spreads from that tiny apex outwards until eventually there is a blessed numbing.

But not for long. A second lubricant or lotion is introduced, my clitoris circled with the stuff, warming it up, and up and up.

'It's getting hotter,' I pant. 'Much hotter now. Really warm. Tingly. Actually, it's nice.' My cunt feels glowy and expanded, a real hot spot. My nipples receive the same treatment and they return to throbbing life.

'You like that?'

'It's kind of intense. I feel really … mmmm.'

My nonsensical ramblings bring his smiling face to where I can see it. He holds up another tub. 'This one I have not used. I think it can be too cruel for today.'

It looks like some kind of hot pepper cream for the treatment of arthritis.

'O say it is good after a spanking. Or bad. It is very painful, she say.'

I stiffen. 'When did you talk to O?'

'When I book the room. Hey, don't look at me like that!'

'Sorry.'

'I make you sorry.' He pretends to open the lid and I repeat my apology, more urgently this time. He puts the tub aside.

My pussy still feels melty-warm and full of need. I hope something very satisfying comes next.

But Dimitri has not tired of teasing me yet. He rubs my nipples with his open palms, very lightly, so that they seem to try to grow to reach him, to climb up to him. Once I am whimpering with need, he moves away and spends ages, real ages, just stroking two fingertips from my breasts to the top of my pubic triangle, over and over and over again, until the magic word is uttered.

'Please.'

'Please? Is something I can do for you?'

'Please don't tease,' I whine.

'No? So what to do instead?'

'Please fuck me.'

'Well, I don't fuck my clients.'

'I'm not your client!'

'I know, but I need to practise for them. So I don't fuck you. But I can do other things.'

'Other …?'

Something starts buzzing. Now I am grateful for the earlier information about Kinky Cupcake's devotion to toy hygiene. All the same, I can't help blurting, 'Is that thing clean?'

'Rosie, it is brand new. Every member has their own labelled vibrator, right? Same with anything that goes inside.'

'Oh, good. Ohhhhh. Goooooood.'

For he has applied the tip to my clit, glancingly at first, then giving it a proper vibration. Deep, deep satisfaction loosens my muscles and sinks into my bones. No more teasing. Proper working to orgasm now.

Except not.

He makes the vibrator perform a delicate dance along the ridges and folds of my labia, never staying in the same place for too long.

I tighten the muscles in my legs, the closest thing to a kick of frustration I can manage in my trussed-up state.

Dimitri laughs and teases, teases and laughs.

'Oh, closer, closer, oh.'

'Like this?' He touches the tip of the vibrator to my clit, so briefly that I almost don't register it, then removes it again.

'No, longer! Keep it there.'

'You are telling me what to do.' He tuts.

'I need you to … please.'

'I like to hear you beg. Can you beg some more?'

The vibrator buzzes, infuriatingly lightly, along my perineum, twirling for one swift revolution in the shallows of my vagina before moving forwards again.

'Please please please please please please.'

The bastard just runs it laconically along the crease of my thighs, close enough for its vibrations to make my labia and clit tingle, but nowhere near close enough to take any of the edge off my desperation.

My voice climbs higher, shriller. 'Dimitriiiii.' It almost cracks.

'You want something?'

'Please let me come.'

'I can do that. If I decide.'

The warmed-up silicone kisses my vagina. It moves down, about half an inch, ready to effect full penetration.

I moan.

He flicks a switch and increases the vibrations. I prepare myself for the big push forwards.

It doesn't happen.

He takes the vibrator back out, leans down and spreads my labia with his finger and thumb so that they are wide apart. He blows a gentle breath on to my clit.

I convulse, spasm with the maddening closeness of my orgasm. 'Noooo.'

He repeats this little torture routine eight times. *Eight times.* My body is weak as water, my legs numb, my wrists sore from the struggle against the cuffs.

I spout a stream of gibberish. 'You can't … no … please … I need to … please let me …'

I am close to tears when he finally shoves the vibrator right inside, adding a thumb to my clit. Three firm thrusts are all it takes to bring me storming into a stars-and-planets blinder of an orgasm.

'Oh God, so cruel, so fucking cruel,' I rave, letting it all gush forth while he holds the buzzing phallus deep inside me and watches.

'OK, nice,' he says, once I've twitched to a halt. 'I make you beg to come. Now I make you beg to stop coming. What about that?'

'What?' I try to raise my head.

He pulls out the vibrator, but it is still on its highest setting, *vrooming* away. He applies it to my clit until it sparks back into life and I can't help trying to grind on it, greedy for my second coming. Once it is fat and full and my vagina sucks hungrily on three of his fingers, he swaps them around, filling my cunt with the smooth, thick silicone cock, pumping it up and down, frigging me with his fingers at the same time. The second climax is even harder than the first and I scream until my voice gives out, stilling to a ragged pant.

'You like this, hmm?'

He doesn't stop fucking me with the vibrator but keeps a smooth pace, slicing it in and out. I feel his hot breath, then his tongue, lapping at my overworked clit. I feel too sensitive there and my thighs try to clamp together, but of course they can't.

'Oh no, it's too much,' I whimper. 'Please stop.'

'Too much?' The words drift over my sex. 'That is for me to say. It is too much when I have enough. I want more of your cunt.'

His mouth closes again over my soaked, over stimulated ripples. He licks and bullies me to a third orgasm, then punishes me with a fourth.

My head disintegrates and my whole body is a marshmallow. I am hot and cold at the same time, my skin slick and clammy. It's like having the flu. He is going to kill me with orgasms.

'You think people will pay for this?'

His voice comes from far away. I can't formulate words. I just grunt.

He pulls out the vibrator from my distended cunt and puts it down.

Next his voice is in my ear and he strokes my hair. 'Rosie. Rosie, are you there?'

I manage to turn my head to him, but my eyelids are heavy and fluttering. I feel drugged.

'Come back, come back.' He brings me slowly into a more recognisable state of consciousness, away from the margins of sleep and dreams. 'Talk to me. Are you OK?'

'I'm OK. So tired. I could sleep – right here.'

'I think this service can be popular,' he says. 'I put it on my menu.'

The word 'menu' is like a finger snapping in my face – it jolts me back into reality. 'Menu? You're like a chef of sex?'

'Yeah, like that. You don't think so? Only one problem I have with this service.'

'What's that?'

He rises from his crouching position, bringing his crotch to my eye level. It bulges to an uncomfortable degree, its denim hardness brushing my cheek.

'Oh, I see. Well, I guess your clients might be OK with helping you out with that.'

'You think?'

'This one might.'

'Oh, really?'

'Really.'

He smiles down at me and starts unbuckling the belts. When his jeans are unbuttoned, his bulge escapes, cock springing out, pointing an accusation at my mouth.

Despite my tethers, I open wide and let the head glide across my cheek and into my mouth via the side of my lips. I can't quite manage the classic blow-job angle from this laid-flat position, but Dimitri slips it in and out of my open orifice while I use my tongue to curl around the tip and tease the sensitive underside.

'Mmm,' he says, taking hold of it at the root and beginning to wank himself into my mouth. I lick and slurp and sometimes succeed in a suck or two, while he bumps against my lips and teeth, moving deeper, deeper, down inside.

Hot salt liquid spurts down my throat and he pumps fast, hips bucking into the side of my head. I swallow his load and lick his shaft clean, worshipping him in the only way I physically can.

He pulls out and drops down to kiss me, long and hard, tongue down where his cock has been, licking and exploring the taste of him.

'You are something,' he says, coming up for air. 'Really something.'

'So are you.'

He unlocks me, lets my boneless legs and arms rest for a while before lifting me off the table and sitting with me on his lap in some kind of bondage chair next to it.

'So then,' he says, after kissing the top of my head. 'You want to try that cross thing next?'

Wheezy laughter pours out of me. 'Maybe next year,' I say.

'Our time is up. We need to put the things we use in a bag and take them to the office.'

I cringe at the thought of handing over our used vibrator and feather tickler to some functionary. 'Can't I take them home and clean them myself?'

'No, they say all toys stay in the building.'

Once my legs work, I dress and leave the dungeon hand in hand with Dimitri, who swings a black plastic bag containing our 'stuff' all the way up the stairs and across the café to the office.

When we knock on the door, the mellifluous tones of O bid us enter. I am a little in awe of her, and I avoid her eye when we walk in.

'Oh, lovely, it's you,' she says with genuine warmth. 'Our two newest members. How did you enjoy your dungeon session? Do sit down, please. If you can.'

She winks at me. I blush and sit heavily on the nearest chair, as if to prove a point.

Dimitri drops the black bag gingerly on her desk. She writes out a tag for it, ties it round the neck and stows it away in a big box.

'All ready for the washer,' she explains. 'So? Do I have to use my imagination about you two in the dungeon? What did you try?'

'A table,' says Dimitri. 'Very interesting design.'

'Well, we do trawl all the best bondage furniture-makers. I like to think we have the most comprehensive stock of any club out there.'

'There is a lot. I hope we try it all.'

'I hope you do,' she says, her smile lingering all over Dimitri's oversized jumper. 'Tell me, do you ever use the café, or come for our social events?'

'I work in evenings,' Dimitri explains. 'Rosie work in daytime.'

'Oh dear, ships that pass in the night. But there's nothing to stop you coming here alone. You're both members. Why not join in and meet a few like-minded people? I'd hate to think you weren't getting the most from your membership here.'

'Oh, I just prefer to be with Dimitri,' I mumble, looking at him sideways to see if he is tempted by this idea. Anton's description of a Dimitri-like man coming out of the door has been drifting around in my head ever since he said the words.

'We are busy people,' he adds, to my distinct pleasure

and relief. 'I try to make career as actor, plus I must learn my English to make it better.'

'What better way to improve your English than by making conversation with native speakers? At social events?'

'Like I say, I am mostly busy. I try to make time, perhaps.'

'Please do. We'd love to see you at one of our group play sessions, for instance. We're all dying to see you in action.'

'Uh-huh, right, well, thank you. Good afternoon.'

He makes his escape, with me in tow, back to the café area, where we buy restorative caffeinated beverages and subside on to the least visible couches.

'We're all dying to see you in action.' I mimic O's nakedly salacious tone, curling my lip. 'Ugh.'

'Is very strange, this O. She make me feel like piece of meat.'

'Poor Dimitri. You're being objectified. Just make sure you don't get exploited next.'

'I think she have plans for us.'

'Plans for you.'

'I don't do no plans without you.'

I glow and melt into the cappuccino froth. 'Aww, really?'

Before he can expand on this statement, a pair of tits with a dog leash dangling in between shoves itself rudely into my line of sight.

It's Turkey Twizzler, and now she's topless, wearing nothing but a teeny latex micro-mini and aforementioned dog leash.

'You really aren't coming to the orgy?' She pouts at Dimitri. 'I've told my handlers you might come. I've wanted to be topped by three men for such a long time. It'd be a dream come true.'

'Handlers?' Dimitri's tone is blank and mystified.

'Tops, you know. Doms. Where are you from? You have the sexiest accent.'

'Moscow,' he says, then picks up his coffee and takes a sip.

'Mmm, so cool. Please come to the orgy. You too.' She turns to me for about a millisecond and casts flat, bored eyes over me.

'Thanks for the invitation,' I reply, unable to keep the sardonic edge out of my voice. 'But no thanks.'

'I don't want group sex,' says Dimitri. 'But thanks also.'

I want to kiss him. In fact, after she shrugs, says, 'Pity,' and turns around to reveal that her skirt has no back other than a wide strap crossing the tops of her thighs, I do.

'That was a very gentlemanly refusal,' I say, staring after her naked arse as it sashays over to the coffee bar where her 'handlers' are waiting for her. 'Most men would want to fuck that.'

'With two others? Not for me. I like a one on one.'

'I thought guys dreamed of having two women at once.'

'Oh well, that's different.'

I elbow him in the ribs. 'How so?'

He ruffles my hair. 'I'm joking. And I am late for work. Come on. I book a room for next Saturday, yes?'

'Of course. Yes.'

Chapter Six

'You're such an enigma these days. It's like I never know what you're thinking about any more.'

'You never did.'

'I thought I did. You thought about the same things I did – music, style, games, films, fun stuff, yeah?'

'Maybe my idea of fun has changed.'

'Has it though? Has it? How?'

Anton leans forwards, his Friday treat gastropub lunch forgotten as he hangs on my next utterance.

'Oh, I dunno. It hasn't really. I can't do tomorrow though. Going to a wedding.'

'Whose?'

'Distant cousin.' My fork freezes halfway to my mouth. Someone I recognise has just entered the pub.

Anton twists his head round, following my line of vision. 'Who's she?'

'Oh, nobody. Who?'

'That woman. Don't pretend you don't know! Your face!'

I shrug and drop my head, hoping that O won't see me.

'Go on – who is she? She's buff.'

'I don't know.'

I can't disguise the wave of visceral loathing that takes me over when Trixietots rocks up at the bar with her, though. I suck my teeth and stab at my pan-fried salmon fillet.

'This is bogus, man,' moans Anton, pushing his plate away. 'You don't talk to me no more. I'm going outside for a smoke, innit. Let me know when you want to be my friend again.'

I sigh. He has a point. I've been lousy company all week. Anton's only crime is his outright failure at being Dimitri, but I can't seem to stop blaming him for it.

In the meantime, I can't stop thinking about my Muscovite partner-in-sin. Wherever I am, I hold imaginary conversations with him. I picture us living a comparatively normal life, going on dates, sitting side by side on sofas, wheeling a trolley around Sainsbury's. What's wrong with me? That's stuff I have never fantasised about in my life. Now I'm getting the whips and chains for real, it's as if my fantasy life has gone into a kind of vanilla switch-over. And besides, I can't even imagine Dimitri sitting still on a sofa for longer than two minutes. He's in a state of perpetual motion, a ball of hairy, bangly energy bouncing around the tennis court of life. Nobody will stop him, least of all me.

If only we could meet more than once a week, though. And if only those meetings could be longer and include other things than experimental kinky sex. Is that a lot to ask? Probably.

I look up from my spring onion and poppy seed mash directly into the fascinated eyes of O and Trixietots.

They pick up their drinks and head over.

Oh God, *go* away.

At least they are clothed, and respectably so, in office wear and discreet make-up.

'Rosie!' O's cultivated, husky tones sound wrong in the middle of this buzzing, noisy pub. 'Do you mind if we come over? Are you on your own?'

'My friend's having a cigarette. He'll be back in a moment.' I try to sound unwelcoming without sounding actually unwelcoming, which isn't easy.

'Oh, we'll move on when he comes back. It's not Dimitri, is it?' Trixietots' eyes gleam with sudden hope.

'No, just a colleague.'

'Is Rosie your real name?' asks O.

'Bit unoriginal.' Trixietots wrinkles her nose. 'We've already got a Rosie Cheeks. And a Rosie Bottom.'

106

'It's my real name.'

'Oh, right. So where's Dimitri?'

'I don't know.'

'So you don't live together?'

'I guess he's sleeping, or working, or hustling theatrical agents. Or playing football. Or something.'

'Theatrical agents? Is he an actor? How did you two meet? If you don't mind my asking.'

Actually, I do. I don't want to assuage your obvious greed for information about the man I love.

'We met in the street,' I tell her. 'It was instant mutual attraction. Eyes meeting across a crowded room and all that. We both felt that fate had thrown us together.'

'How romantic,' says O, after a pause that seems to contain some scepticism. 'And how long have you been together?'

'About three months. Ish.' I try to calculate how long we have actually known each other, then add it to the six weeks Dimitri claimed at our 'interview'.

'Oh?' O looks puzzled. 'Dimitri said four when we spoke at the room booking.'

'Yeah, well, the attraction was instant, but we didn't act on it instantly. There was a gap between our eyes meeting and other parts meeting.'

Trixietots grins. 'You're exclusive?'

'Oh yes.'

'Such a shame. I want you at one of our orgies. Both of you. Couldn't you be persuaded?'

'Oh, I don't think so.'

'At least ask him. Ask Dimitri for us. We'll plan it around when you're both free. It doesn't have to be at the dead of night. Just come and watch if you don't feel comfortable with joining in.'

'My friend's coming back now.' I flap my hands at them, shooing them off.

'Ask him,' O says again before heading back to the bar.

'So you do know them.' Anton's tone is accusatory.

'Oh, just leave it. Just forget it, OK? I'm going back to work.'

* * *

'Dimitri,' I say, nervous, blowing on the foam of my cappuccino.

'Yes?'

'This secret life thing. I'm not sure it's for me. People keep asking me what I'm doing on Saturday afternoon. I'm in danger of losing friends.'

'Why? What you tell them? You are having kinky sex with a bad Russian man?'

'No.' I burst out laughing despite myself, disturbing the froth so it blows over onto the table.

108

'Well, is easy enough. You say you are with a boyfriend. What is wrong with that?'

'I'm not comfortable with lying.'

I look him up and down, his tall lean figure arranged in a relaxed posture, legs out in front, one elbow crooked with a hand behind his head. My mouth waters.

'What is the lie? I am not your boyfriend?' He sounds put out. My heart zings.

'Are you? Are you my boyfriend?'

'I think so. You don't?'

'Yes, yes, I do. I want to. I didn't know.'

'You have sex with me, I don't pay you, you like it. This to me is girlfriend.'

'That's good. I just wondered if you saw it as some kind of business arrangement or something.'

He stretches the crooked arm, rests it behind my neck, hand on my shoulder. His fingertips ruffle my hair at the side of my head.

'If all business arrangements was like this, the world is a better place,' he opines, grinning. Then he puts his head to one side, his eyes suddenly cast down and serious. 'I'm sorry I only see you once a week. You understand I am so busy working in this kitchen. And then I must look for acting job. And then I must see my housemates who are my cousins. Soon we will make more time, I promise.'

I almost burst with love for him. I reach out and stroke his cheek. 'I'd like that. I really would.'

He takes my hand and kisses the fingers. All meaning detaches from time and space.

'Oh,' he says, 'I forget. I promise O we will go watch her friends have sex after we finish in boudoir.'

'What?'

'Before you arrive, O ask me if we have time to watch this orgy. I start work at six, is only two now. So I say yes. What's wrong? I only try to be polite. Is English to be polite, right?'

I squeeze his fingers. 'I know. I just think O and her friends have designs on you.'

'Designs?'

'They want to get their hands on you.'

'Ah. Ha ha. You think they are having lust for me?'

'Definitely. Much lust. I think they want you to join in the orgy.'

'Ah.'

'I mean, if you wanted to ...' I hold my breath.

'Is not why I come here.'

'No. Me neither. But ...'

'You want to have sex with these people?'

'No.'

'OK. I don't too. But I promise we watch, so ...'

'It's fine. We'll watch.'

* * *

An hour later, after Dimitri has tied me up beautifully in ribbons, like a package, using instructions from a book, then done depraved things to me – some painful, some not – on a four-poster bed, we relax in the boudoir, waiting for company.

'Is quite a form of art, this type of bondage,' he comments, releasing me from my silken cocoon so that I can dress in time for the performance. 'It take a long time though. Maybe too long to put on my menu. We hardly have time for sex fun today.'

True. I pout a little, but I did at least get one orgasm out of it.

'Next time we do easy bondage, get more sex, I think.'

It was sex enough, I thought with pleasurable reminiscence, to have his strong hands wrap me round and round in satiny ribbon until I lay helpless beneath his touch. I could do that again. And again.

He passes me my dress, an easy slip-on jersey number, perfect for this kind of leisure activity. I've hardly got my head through the neck hole when there is a knock at the door. *Them.*

We hop off the bed together and I go to sit on a chintzy chaise longue while Dimitri opens the door.

'Dimitri!' Trixietots launches herself on to him, hanging off his neck, crushing her ample tits against his chest.

'So, so glad you could come. And I hope you will! Tee-hee!' Giggle, flirt, hair twirl, finger suck. Stupid cow. 'You'll want to join in, I know it. Can't wait!'

He manages to detach her and gives her hand a gallant kiss. She looks over at me and nods unenthusiastically. After her, two men – the 'handlers' – troop in, then O and Mal bring up the rear.

Dimitri joins me on the chaise, bundling me up close and sitting me on his lap. This could be interesting, I think, as the folds of my skirt fall away and my bare thighs rest on his patchy jeans. Maybe I could just sleep through the whole thing, using Dimitri's chest as a handy pillow.

My interest is piqued, however, when Mal and the handlers sit like three solemn jurors on the end of the bed, watching O and Trixietots, who stand before them.

'Strip,' orders Mal, and the two women immediately comply.

Trixietots has little to shed, just a skimpy vest top and denim micro-mini that barely covers her rounded arse. O, on the other hand, is layered in jackets, waistcoats, blouses, skirts, slips.

Eventually, both stand in heels and underwear – Trixietots in white stilettos, a white latex thong and sparkly pasties, O in a sheer black lace basque and suspenders but no knickers at all. O is tall and straight and slender as a willow wand in her shiny black pumps.

Trixie looks like a cover model for *Booty or Bust* magazine, all fake ash-blonde hair and lip gloss.

'Which would you choose?' I whisper to Dimitri.

'I don't know,' he says.

'Let's start with some girl on girl,' decrees Mal. 'O, I want you to sit down on that chair, spread your legs and let Trix lick you out. Oh, but first, make out together, by all means.'

Trixie and O curl into each other and fall to smooching. Trixie is like an overenthusiastic puppy, wrapping her thigh around O's delicate waist, snuffling and biting as the kiss gets more serious.

Hard flesh dents my bare bottom. Dimitri is enjoying the show.

Their hands are everywhere, Trixie's blood-red vamp nails, O's square-cut French manicured ones, patting bottoms, grazing thighs, squeezing breasts.

O falls backwards onto the chair, toppling Trixie in her wake. Trixie collapses onto her knees between O's thighs and kisses them ravenously.

'I can't see your cunt, O,' says Mal, and she widens her legs to oblige the audience. 'Trixie, spread her lips. Get your head out of the way – we want to see.'

I watch the three men remove their cocks from their trousers and wrap them around with eager fists while Trixie sets to work. She overacts atrociously like a person in a bad porn movie, but I can't take my eyes off O, who seems like the still centre of the room, drawing and absorbing attention, making a flicker of the eyelid count twenty times more than Trixie's stagey moans.

When she comes, she simply puts her hands on Trixie's head and leans forwards, shutting her eyes, exhaling with such control that you imagine she'd blow a great series of smoke rings. She must have practised this skill of the silent orgasm – I just don't know how that's done.

'Gorgeous,' says one of the handlers. He turns to his companion. 'Who's having Trix first – me or you?'

Trixie sits back on her heels, looks directly over at us and licks her lips, pulling a face of exaggerated sultriness. I roll my eyes, then look at Dimitri, who seems ... I don't know. I don't think he's terribly impressed anyway.

The handler who spoke gets up and hauls Trixie to her feet, but not for long. Quick as a flash, she is bent over the end of the bed, thong ripped down and cock inserted. I cringe a little, hoping she is at least ready. The handler goes to it with frightening speed, crushing her into the wooden bed frame.

I turn my attention away from the blur of motion to where O stands between Mal and the other handler. Mal has a bendy kind of whip thing that he draws on O's stomach with, making swirly shapes while the handler holds her arms flat against her sides from behind.

What Mal is doing is undoubtedly interesting, but the thing I can't take my eyes from is O's face. She is present and yet absent. When Mal flicks the whip over her breasts and then down between her thighs, I wince, but she doesn't. She half shuts her eyes and sighs out a breath. Her lips are full and her cheeks flushed, but there's something so odd about her. She is in a state of rapture, I think, on a different plane of consciousness.

The handler puts his hand between her legs, rubbing between her labia while Mal continues to whip her breasts, raising welts on the tender flesh. I watch fascinated, even though breast whipping is probably never going to be my thing. Perhaps, I think, it isn't her thing either, but the way she looks at Mal makes me think that she will do anything for him, no matter what. Is this the way your dom is meant to make you feel? Would I do this for Dimitri?

The handler pushes her to her knees and bends her head over Mal's cock. She sucks it as if it is a holy relic, worshipping it. The handler scrambles down behind her, parts her arse cheeks and then pushes his cock into her cunt.

She sucks and fucks while Trixie and her man, long since spent, watch and make coarse remarks. While O's body bends and flexes to the will of the two men who control it, I wonder if I'll ever be such a perfect sub. Dimitri is uncomfortably hard underneath me. It occurs to me that he'll need to deal with that before he goes to work. Could we just leave, mid-orgy, and find some bolthole for a quickie?

'Come and join in,' says Trixie, grinning over at us. 'There's plenty of room.'

My breath hitches as I wait for Dimitri to answer.

'I don't think so. But thanks.'

I twist my neck around to catch his eye. 'Do you want to go?' I whisper. 'Find somewhere private?'

He nods, then stands up.

O has just swallowed Mal's load and the handler seems to be reaching the end of his road too. As for O, she seems to be floating between them, serene and untouched in her happy place.

Dimitri clears his throat. The men and Trixie look over, but O doesn't seem to notice. 'We have to go,' he says. 'Thank you for interesting experience. Goodbye.'

Outside, as soon as the door is shut, I can't help giggling like a lunatic, especially when Dimitri bundles me towards a dark corner of the corridor where a curtain is drawn over a niche containing an attic window.

'OK,' he whispers. He kisses me, then he spins me round and bends me so my palms rest on the windowsill. 'Keep still and don't make a sound.'

I bounce on the soles of my feet, knowing what to expect but still having to suppress a little whimper of delight when my dress goes up and my knickers come down. The familiar snap of rubber is followed by the cherished nudge of cock on cunt, then the splitting swoop forwards, parting my muscles with ease, gliding in on a wave of my juices. He holds me by the breasts, cupping them firmly while he thrusts. His thumbs stroke my nipples under my dress, hardening them.

'You want I whip your tits?' he whispers. 'You want that?'

Rationally speaking, the answer is 'no'. But something about watching O in the boudoir has inspired me, showed me something about real submission.

So instead I say, 'I want you to do whatever you want with me.'

He pushes in to the hilt and holds himself there, his breath wavering. 'You really? You mean that?'

'Whatever you want. I'm yours.'

His fingers work on my nipples with furious speed while he fucks me harder, into the wall, making my knees bend with every thrust.

'You turn me on,' he says, at least I think that's what he says. I'm starting to blow my lid, the steam rising. 'I make you come so hard.'

'You do, you do.' He does, he does. My knees give way and only his cock holds me in place while he works himself to his orgasm, pinning me to the windowsill, gasping and grabbing me hard in his effort not to make too much noise.

I wriggle joyfully on the end of his cock, wanting it to stay, regretting its departure when he slides it out and slumps down on his knees next to me, brow on the sill.

'Whatever I want, hey?' he says when he turns his face to the side and catches my eyes in a drugged, heavy-lidded gaze.

I'm light-headed, cutting through the thousand qualifiers that spring to mind to answer with a simple, 'Yes.'

It's a risk, perhaps a huge and dangerous risk, but somehow it doesn't feel like one at all.

Chapter Seven

Whatever he wants.

Whatever that might be.

I spend the week contemplating the possibilities. There are so many that I make myself dizzy.

He might want a full-time slave or he might want a no-strings Saturday shag. He might want to throttle me during sex, like that couple I'd seen on TV once, or he might want to watch while a procession of men in leather fuck me in turn.

There really aren't any limits to what he might want. A lot of it is frightening, but then I catch myself and tell myself that I'm just trying to spook myself, like when I used to imagine all the bad things that could happen to me between my house and school. I fear the worst so that

119

I'm prepared for it. It doesn't mean it's going to happen.

I just wish I *knew* him. I wish we could just *talk* sometimes.

'How was the wedding?' asks Anton, catching me off guard.

'What wedding?'

'Exactly.' He pronounces the word with savage satisfaction, trying to hold my eye accusingly. But I'm not in the mood for accusations, so I shrug and offer to make tea for the rest of the office.

He doesn't invite me anywhere this weekend.

I am more on tenterhooks than ever for my regular Saturday tryst with Dimitri. Looking for clues as to our probable activities, I text him a question.

'What should I wear?'

He replies: 'Whatever you want.'

This isn't helpful. It's what *he* wants that I need to know, have to know, will die of fretting pretty soon if I don't find out.

I text back: 'Spacesuit then?'

'If you like.'

Of course, I don't have a spacesuit. In the end I go with my usual flirty dress with stockings. I feel so drab amongst the wet-look man-made materials in the café, though, especially beside Dimitri who is more like a one-man carnival than ever, trailing scarves and fringes in his jingly-jangly wake.

'So then,' I quaver, ridiculously nervous, my coffee cup jittering in my hand.

'So then,' he prompts when I don't continue. His smile is playful, his eyes only pretend stern.

'Just wondering what's on the menu for today.'

'Your choice,' he says. Why all these curve balls? Can't he act predictably, just once?

'My choice? Dinner at the Ivy then?'

He chuckles and tickles me under the chin. 'One day, I promise you. But tonight must be something we do in the schoolroom, because I have booked there. You can choose what. I have one rule.'

'A rule? What's the rule?'

'What you choose, you must not have done it before.'

'Well, that covers quite a lot of things.'

'And it is maybe something you never planned to do. Something maybe that scares you.' His fingertip rests beneath my chin, holding up my head, keeping my eyes fixed on his.

My scalp begins to crawl with dread anticipation. He wants me to do something that scares me. All my anxious fantasies of the past week crowd into my mind.

'Why?' I ask weakly. 'Why something that scares me?'

His hand moves around to cradle my shoulder, putting me in an instantly reassuring place. 'Because I want to make it good for you. Take your fear and kill it.'

'Maybe it won't be possible.'

'If it is, I will do it. Think of a scary thing. Tell me what it is.'

I try to calm my thoughts, to come up with a workable list.

Nothing with multiple partners, for a start. That's a scary step too far, just for now. Piercing? I picture Dimitri looming above me with a needle and a lighter flame ... no. No way. My imagination takes me on a whistle-stop tour of all the most outrageous sexual practices I have ever heard of before coming to a sudden stop as something infinitely more simple, more doable, more intimate and yet just as scary occurs to me.

'There is something,' I say slowly, then I stop. I don't know if I can say the words.

'Good. So what is it?'

I hide my face in his shoulder. 'I can't tell you.'

'Ohhh,' he croons, delighted by my reticence, grabbing my hair and making me look at him. 'You can't tell me? Is it very bad? Very, very wicked? I hope so.'

'I don't think it's that uncommon, actually,' I say. 'I guess lots of people do it. Just, I can't imagine it feeling good. Not for, y'know, maybe for the person giving it, not so much for the person receiving.'

I really, really hope all my hedging and skirting is giving him a clue. I just don't want to say the words out loud: they are so ugly, so bald, so crude.

'You mean the cane?' He frowns.

'Nooo. Nothing to do with spanking. Something a bit more … intimate. I imagine it can be painful, all the same. And it does involve the same … body part.'

'Ah!' His bangles clash as inspiration strikes. 'You mean anal sex, right?'

Was there any need to say it *quite* so loudly and emphatically? A number of people at neighbouring tables look over and smirk. I curl back up into the crook of Dimitri's arm, pressing up close to his rangy, bony shoulder, suppressing an urge to whimper with embarrassment.

'My God, why are you so shy about this?' He hugs me tight, half laughing. 'Is very common, I think. I suppose everybody here has done it, yes? Hey, look at me, stop hiding.'

But I only shake my head, forehead rubbing his shirt. He pinches the back of my neck and I squint up at him. 'Can I change my mind?'

'No,' he says, but then he softens. 'You really want to?'

The speck of disappointment in his voice nerves me. 'No, no, it's OK. I'll do it.'

'*We'll* do it. You aren't alone.' He takes my hands and squeezes them. I can't help but smile at him. I don't know if your dom is supposed to make you smile as much as he does. Shouldn't I be cowering or something? 'Let's go,' he whispers.

We walk through a barrage of grins and whispers and

I flush furious scarlet, imagining everyone watching my backside as I pass, knowing what's in store for it.

I shudder slightly on the stairs, tensing my sphincter muscles in readiness.

'You've done it before, I presume?'

'Oh yeah. Of course.'

The fact that it's no big deal for him is both comforting and alienating.

'I mean, you really *have* done it? Not like when you told Mal and O you'd had a ton of submissives?'

'I don't lie to you, Rosie. With other people, I am acting. With you, I am myself.'

'That's … Oh, that's really nice. That's so sweet.'

'What about you? You are yourself with me?'

We are at the schoolroom door now, ready to enter.

'Never more so,' I say, meaning it.

'Good.'

The schoolroom is cold, but Dimitri has a solution for that involving lips and tongues and wandering hands. When the hands wander under my skirt and find my lace-covered bottom, I shiver and tense.

He breaks off, resting his forehead on mine. 'This really is scary for you? Why?'

'I think it will hurt.'

'I use lube. Lots of it.'

'All the same, I don't see how something that size can ever fit.'

'You are not made of wood, *malyshka*. You stretch. Like a rubber.'

My entire body convulses with dread.

'To talk will not help,' he decides. He peers around the room. 'I wish I book the boudoir. This room not so comfortable for anal sex.'

Do you need special furniture then? He drags out a padded bench, like something from a school gymnasium, and removes one of the wooden blocks, lowering its height. 'This may be OK,' he says, stroking his chin. 'You take off your dress and lie down.'

I stare at the makeshift bed.

'Lie down, Rosichka,' he says, unbendingly.

'The thing is,' I pipe, half turning, voice shaking. 'You wouldn't do this with a client, would you? So should you be …?'

'I do this with clients but I use plugs. Only difference, with you I use my cock. But if you like, I can use a plug instead.'

'No.' I surprise myself with the speed and conviction of my reply. 'Don't use plugs. I want you. If I'm going to do this, I want it to be with you. Not some object.'

'OK. So then …' He flaps his hands, as if to ask why I'm still clothed.

I set about pulling my dress over my head while he inspects the contents of the front desk. He finds what he is looking for – a bottle of lubricant – and pops it in his shirt pocket. Then he is behind me, his hands over my upper arms, his lips on my neck.

'You are my brave Rosichka,' he says. His hands scoop up my breasts in their flimsy bra, kneading them gently. The tingle transfers, slowly but inexorably, from my nipples to my clit. I push my bottom back into his crotch, feeling it harden. 'You give me your ass, I will treat it well, hmm. You trust me?'

I am boneless in his arms, belonging to him already. 'Yes.'

'OK.' He finds my mouth, dips into it with his tongue until I am hot and panting, keeping up the pressure on my nipples, grinding his pelvis into my bottom. 'Now you are going to lie down on that thing, OK. I help you.'

I want him inside me, but not like that. I want to trick him into my pussy instead. While he aids me into the required position – stomach flat on the padding, legs dangling over the side, bottom up at the edge of the seat – I make plans.

My plans are probably a bit lame. I spread my legs and try to raise my pussy to his line of sight, but it's already too late. He has taken the bottle from his shirt pocket with one hand while the other strokes my back and shoulder blades with his knuckles.

'You can relax,' he says, deep and low. 'Relax and float away.'

He puts the lube down on a desk and moves both

hands to my stretch-lacy bum cheeks, massaging them for a while before pulling down and removing the knickers. He goes back to the massage. It really does feel gorgeously sensual. I want him to carry on indefinitely, and yet I also want him to move lower, find my clit, find my cunt, use them.

'Getting wet,' he says. 'Getting ready.'

The word 'ready' makes me tense again, barricading the passage.

He taps my bottom, very lightly, but with a purposeful authority that I have to respect. 'No, that is not right. Don't tense. Relax the muscles.'

Struggling slightly, I obey, glad he can't see my grimace of effort.

He parts my cheeks with his thumbs. I inhale sharply, panicking at the sense of exposure. I can't hide this secret any more. He has it in his sights. And what if he is disgusted by it? What if it turns him off and he makes his excuses and changes course?

This has been the fear, much more than any pain or discomfort it might involve. The real fear of losing him.

'Hello,' he says. I feel his breath, warm in that intimate furrow, telling me that Dimitri has bent his head and is close to his target. 'Here we are. Let's get you ready.'

I let out the breath. No disgust there. Just avid lust. Dimitri won't be going anywhere, and neither will I until he has taken that last bastion of my ever-fading virtue. I squirm with sudden shameful joy at the thought.

My arse is his.

He removes his hands and I hear the uncapping of the bottle. I can't seem to stop swaying my hips from side to side, enjoying the slight friction of the smoothed suede under my stomach.

'Hey, keep still.' He lets a lubed thumb glide between my cheeks. 'Don't move a muscle.' He says this last in a deliberate American accent, which comes off exaggerated and wrong, but I still picture him in a cowboy hat, ready to aim and fire. 'Now enjoy.'

He runs slippery fingers up and down the crease, pressing into my inner cheeks, an act that releases startlingly pleasant sensations. My muscles seem to tremble and twitch a little, as if they know what's coming. In a way, perhaps, they do. This kind of stimulation has an inevitable purpose. Does it trigger ancient human memories for them? The cavewoman, worn out with childbearing, offering her caveman an alternative? The wife of a Roman senator, jealous of his preference for boys? Or the woman through the ages, wanting her man to know her in every possible way? This act is as old as the hills, and practised only for pleasure, not for any other motive. People do it because they want each other, just like me and Dimitri.

Now I am calm and lulled by the idea of all my

forerunners opening this part of themselves up to their lovers as an act of faith and trust. It's nothing new. It's safe, as long as I'm in the right hands. And I'm in the right hands.

'Now you feel this,' he murmurs, bending to my ear. I tighten my muscles as one cold fingertip circles dangerously close. 'How does it feel?'

'Oh, nice,' I say. 'But it's so close. I'm worried.'

'Don't worry, hush. Keep it open, relax.'

The fingertip is on me now, ready for the first push forwards. I think about asking him to put more lube on it, but then I force myself to trust him. He knows what he's doing. Let him do it.

I can't hold back a tiny whimper, though, as my ring stretches to accommodate the end of that long slim finger. I pant quickly, the breaths high up in my chest, trying to quantify the unique feeling of penetration. It's not like having a finger in my pussy. It feels bigger, stranger and a little uncomfortable, though not at all painful as yet.

'I am in you,' he says, curling it a little, swivelling it, feeling his way.

I unleash a manic giggle, flexing my ankles and feet, experiencing something akin to being tickled, but not quite.

He digs deeper, sliding in to the knuckle.

'All the way,' he says in a sing-song croon. 'All the way inside. Oh yes. You can take it.'

'Ugh, ugh, ugh,' is my only response to this. It's not painful, not even unpleasant. It just feels very *wrong*, like my body and his finger are in deadlocked opposition. But he will win.

While his finger wiggles in its new home, he kisses my captive bum cheeks, passionately, then he pretends to bite them, sucking marks on to their pristine pallor.

'Oooh.' I grip the worn suedette with desperate nails. I know I can't come like this, but it feels weirdly as if I might. Maybe all the information is wrong?

Then, with a rude pop, his finger is out of me and my muscles contract as if offended by his sudden exit.

'Oh.' It's a little moan of protest, and he knows it, for the next thing he does is to insert two fingers. This makes me open my eyes wide and kick up my heels, but he is firm in his intent and he continues his impaling mission until I feel that pain I have been dreading. But it's not really the dreaded pain – it's a pale shadow of it, a vague smarting halfway along the passage, which flares and then as quickly fades.

How does the width of two fingers compare with his cock? I find myself trying to perform a frantic estimation task in my head. His fingers are long and bony, his cock is long and not so bony. Quite thick, in fact. How much more will it hurt? What's the factor?

He thrusts with the fingers for a while, letting me accustom myself to the invasive feel of them, the push in and the drag out, then I hear his breathing over mine and it is heavy, ragged, on the edge.

'I take you now,' he says. I shut my eyes and utter a silent prayer, pushing up my bottom, offering it. 'But you must turn over. Lie on your back. I want to watch your face.'

'Oh no!' This really is beyond the pale. He can put what he likes up my bum, but he mustn't look at my face while he does it! Nobody must ever see my face.

'What?' He removes his fingers, comes around to the side, seeks my eyes, which are pressed into the padding. 'Look at me. Hey, Rosichka. Now.'

I turn a pouty face to his. 'It's too embarrassing.'

'But I need to see you. Or you might be in horrible pain and I don't know. You might hate every minute and I think you love it. This is important for me, to know that you are happy with how I fuck you.'

'If I'm not, I'll tell you.'

I know before I even say it that he won't accept that though.

'But will you, *malyshka*? I am not so sure.'

He has a point. I probably wouldn't say anything, just let him pound away and keep my fingers crossed that he would come quickly. It occurs to me that I could learn a thing or two about honesty from Dimitri.

'OK. I don't know what I'll do, to be fair. It's a new experience, after all.'

'So you turn over for me, please.'

'I turn over for you.'

I have to hop off the gymnastics horse and then seat myself on it again. My rear cheeks squish and slide together, the lube at work. I'm also aware of feeling different, the after-effects of Dimitri's fingering. The passage remains tight, but I know it can take an invasive presence. All the old jokes about anal probes run through my mind as I lie flat and peer up at Dimitri through almost-closed eyes.

He picks up my legs from their dangling position and puts them over his shoulders, then holds me by my hips, angling me so that my bum rises right off the surface. Watching my face intently, he applies more lubricant to my quivering pucker.

I shut my eyes, bite my lip.

'This is not hurting you?'

'No, no.' I gasp the words out, ruffling his hair with my toes.

'Good. Please to open your eyes. I must watch you.'

He is evil. I reconsider all my opinions of him. Kind, funny, sweet, sexy all turn to evil, evil, evil, evil.

I manage to unglue one eyelid and squint up at him. 'Whyyyy?' I wail.

'Because I like to.' That smile makes lightning flash to my crotch. His fingertips press against my bud. I watch the way his forearm twists and his wrist flexes in the commission of my anal preparation, then I look up at his face again. His eyes are alight, his cheekbones twitching, his forehead drawn with the effort of concentration.

'I will do it now,' he says. He drops his jeans quickly and rubbers up with ruthless efficiency. I watch him stroke more lube onto the tip of his latex-sheathed cock. It is coming for me, coming to get me. Against the advice, I tense.

He obviously feels my calves and thighs tighten against his body and shakes his head at me. 'Relax now,' he says, gently admonitory.

I let my shoulders drop and the rest of my body follows suit. I centre all my focus on keeping my rear muscles ready.

Holding his cock in one hand, while the other keeps me raised at the hip, he steps forwards. The blunt tip parts my cheeks further; he rubs it up and down the cleft, gathering more lubricant. The way he looms over me, like a dark conqueror, is both scary and arousing. I sense my vulnerability and I embrace it, let it wash over me, experience it as pleasure instead of fear.

When he lines himself up with my opening I can't help the involuntary clench of my sphincter. He soothes me out of it, shushing and stroking until my body obeys me and my dread of the first push forwards turns to acceptance.

'Oh!' I yelp and shut my eyes, trying to process the feeling of having my arsehole stretched and filled.

'Hey, hey, open them. I need to see you.'

His insistence on this makes me want to resist and misbehave, but he holds himself perfectly still until I do as he asks and glare at him through lowered lashes.

'This is hurting you now?'

'Not really. I don't know. It's weird.'

'I push some more?'

I nod my head and turn it to the side, acutely coy. His forward motion rips through me and I can't help but cry out and try to expel the invader. He holds me firm.

'This pain is soon over, I promise.'

'It's OK, you can go on, I just … my body does things I don't ask it to.'

I can't work out whether I want him to continue penetrating me or not. I just can't seem to fix the cost/benefit analysis in place. It hurts, but it's hot. I love the idea of being taken like this, but the reality is a little bit raw. My brain wants him in me, but my arsehole – not so much.

I breathe through the momentary panic, then he eases slowly onwards. The spasm of revulsion my body went through passes, and the pain, so hot and sharp at first, evens out to a manageable throb.

I start to like it.

But I still don't want to look at him, except from the extreme corner of my eye.

134

At last he is there, all the way in. I feel distended and full to bursting, my stomach a little crampy, but the knowledge of what I have let him do to me is intoxicating and I want to float away on a wave of submission.

'I am in your ass,' he says, somewhat unnecessarily. Does he think I haven't noticed? He's clearly only saying it so he gets to use that victorious tone. 'I like it here. What about you?'

'I feel so full,' I whisper.

'Yeah, you are. Full of my cock. In your ass.' I do know that, Dimitri. 'Now, look at me in the eye.'

'I can't.'

He does something with his hips, and I feel an extra little jab inside my darkest, deepest passage. 'You can.'

I do it. The enormous intimacy of the moment almost undoes me. He bends and stretches to kiss me, a feathery, gentle thing that he holds for as long as it takes me to fight back the tears.

'OK,' he whispers, moving slowly back to a straight posture. 'Now you watch me while I fuck your ass, yes?'

'Yes, sir,' I sigh. I am at the point of no return. I can't let this end now.

He starts slowly, making me feel every millimetre of his cock as it drags itself back then returns to my tight embrace. It is such a large sensation, it completely engulfs me. I can't possibly think of anything else while I'm being buggered except the fact of buggery. The hot, sweet, dirty truth of it. The stretch of advance, the clench of retreat, the constant sting, the intense feeling of occupation.

My vision smudges around the edges, blurring his face. I watch his lower abdomen and pelvis rush to meet me then pull back, forwards, back. I can't see his cock, but I can certainly feel it, and I can see him let go of my hip with one of his hands and move it to my clit.

'Oh!'

He looks like the devil, grinning through the sweat, taking his moment of triumph and drawing it out indefinitely.

I am finished, defeated, taken, mastered. It takes no more than a cursory rub of my button to make my passage tighten and spasm around his cock – I feel the quake as a series of strong vibrations, tearing through me from the back to the front. My vagina, unoccupied, ripples in sympathy as if begging for a cock of its own.

Dimitri yells, 'Yes!' and shoves himself in and out with less ceremony, his thrusts hard and almost brutal. 'You come with me in your ass, baby! Now I give you it.'

His speed makes me writhe and kick, but he doesn't let up.

'You get this often, believe it,' he vows. 'Your ass is mine now.'

I am making incoherent little sounds, not quite words but a bit more than yelps when he digs his fingers into my hips and hisses his way through a long, apparently fierce, orgasm.

Slapping himself once, twice, three times right up inside me while his eyes roll back, he says something in Russian then releases my hips and lets me loll against him, still impaled, while he kisses each of my calves. then rests his damp forehead against one of my legs, gathering breath.

'I'm sorry,' he says after a while.

'You're sorry?' I raise my head and peer at him. He looks so sad. 'Hey, Dimitri! What for?'

'In the end, it takes over me. I forget to make sure you are OK. I think maybe I hurt you?'

'No.' I prop myself on my elbows and lock my ankles behind his neck, rubbing them into his flesh caressingly. 'Well, yeah. A bit. But no more than I could handle. It stopped hurting after a while anyway. I got used to it, I guess. My body adjusted.'

'You really are OK? You don't think I am terrible boyfriend?'

I laugh, slightly tearfully. 'God, no. I think you are wonderful boyfriend. The best.'

A watery smile turns up the corners of his lips. 'You are the best,' he says gallantly. He pauses to remove his softened cock, with infinite care and tenderness, from my thoroughly fucked bum. His absence feels as wrong as his presence did. My anus protests, reaching after him. I try to sit up but I'm too weak.

He removes the condom, ties it in a knot and aims it, deadly accurate, at the wastepaper basket. Then he moves my legs down so they encircle his waist and picks me up, holding me close and tight in his arms until we both subside onto the floor in a tangle of limbs.

It's not comfortable down there, but we don't care. Besides, there's nowhere else we can do this in the austere schoolroom. The dusty floor will have to do.

'You know, although that was incredibly hot and dirty and nasty and all that, there was something incredibly romantic about it too,' I tell him.

'You think so?'

'Yeah. Because you were so concerned about getting it right – for my sake. It was really ... gah. I hate all this soppy talk. But it was really touching, you know? I felt cared for.' *Loved*. But I'm not going to presume.

'Well, you are, you know?' he says, hugging the breath from my lungs. 'You are my favourite thing in England.'

'Really? You're my favourite Russian thing. Even better than vodka.'

'Wow, that is amazing compliment, I thank you.' He kisses my brow, chuckling under his breath. 'I take you to Moscow one day.'

'I'd like that.'

'How is your ass?'

The change of subject foxes me for a moment, until I realise he is enquiring about my recently sodomised orifice.

'A bit tender,' I tell him. 'But I like that. I like to feel that bad things have been done to me. A reminder.'

'I will remember it also,' he says. 'I will think of it a lot, until I see you again.'

'Next Saturday?'

'I guess. Shit. I don't want to go to work. But I must make the money. We have to go.'

'What's next?'

'I put you on that cross and I whip you, baby.'

'I'll look forward to it.'

Chapter Eight

'There's that guy again.'

Anton is leaning against the wall, secret-agent style, looking sideways through the office window.

'What guy?'

'The brothel guy, or whatever that place is.'

'I'm sorry.' I look up from my radio ad copy and attempt to pay the increasingly irritating Anton some of the attention he clearly craves. 'What?'

'Every day this week I've seen the same dude go in there. Pretty early in the morning for a sex fiend. I reckon he's a sex addict, must be.'

'Why do you think it's a brothel? Might be a crack den.'

'No way, there's no way it's a crack den. Those people

140

aren't crack heads. Besides, who heard of a crack den that's open in the morning?'

'Perhaps it's a … I dunno … creative arts space or something.'

'Too many suits. This guy might fit that profile though. He definitely looks artistic. Meaning weird.'

'Does he?' I humour him, wanting to get our friendship back on its old footing. 'What kind of weird?'

'He looks like someone from the Moscow State Circus or something. And with the best porn tache I've ever seen.'

I leap out of my chair and join him at the window, nausea rising in my throat.

'Where? Let me see.'

'He's gone in now. I'll let you know when he comes out.'

'So you're going to stand there all day? What about the Trufax account?'

'Ah, yeah, forgot about that. Oh, and I've seen her before. She goes in there pretty much every day.'

O is wearing a beige trench coat, belted at the waist, and a beret. She looks like a caricature Frenchwoman. The dark glasses, on a day of low November cloud, complete the impression.

'Do you think she's one of the hookers?'

'Could be. That blonde that went in earlier deffo is. High heels, fishnets, the works, at nine fifteen in the morning.'

I thought Trixietots had a day job. What would she be doing there? And is Dimitri with them? And if so, why hasn't he told me about it?

'Blonde?'

'Yeah. Blonde. You're interested again?'

'Course I'm interested.'

'It's just that you haven't seemed that bothered lately. Considering how obsessed you used to be with that place. Tell you what, why don't we go down and stake it out at lunchtime? Like we did that time in the summer.'

'We didn't find anything out,' I remind him, every fibre of my being uneasy.

'Not that time.'

'Nah, it's OK. It's too cold for hanging around the streets anyway.'

'Oh! There she is again – the blonde!'

I peer over his shoulder. Trixietots emerges from the black door, swathed in a fake-fur coat, hair swept up and full make-up in place, looking like anything but a sober-suited City worker.

I almost want to close my eyes and pretend I haven't seen anything.

Especially when Dimitri follows her out.

'That's the guy I was telling you about!'

But I can't reply. All I can do is stare bleakly as he pauses in the covered arch above the door to light a cigarette. Trixietots turns around and says something, laughing. He inclines his head, flirtatiously if you ask me, takes a drag on the cigarette and winks at her. They turn their backs to me and disappear around the corner of the street.

'Weird-looking guy, right? Who the hell has a moustache like that these days?'

'I need the loo.'

I spend ten minutes kneeling with my head over the toilet bowl, dizzy, my heart wrenched out of place.

Why? How? Why? How? The questions keep repeating themselves in a loop while the hard tiles bruise my knees.

Eventually the rushing, roaring sensation subsides and I am able to function, if minimally. I take my phone from my handbag and stare at it, as if I've forgotten what it is.

What should I do?

I feel I have to speak to him. Now. I dial his number, trying to work out what I'm going to say and not succeeding overmuch.

It goes to voicemail.

I try again.

Voicemail again. His phone is switched off. He always switches it off for our 'sessions'.

My head swims with indecision. An impulse forms, quickly, and before I can question it I am heading down the back stairs and out of the building.

I approach Kinky Cupcake from the least visible street corner, scurrying in past the lone morning bouncer, who tilts his head and looks at me with unabashed curiosity. I am hoping that Anton has relinquished his post and is actually getting some work done.

'Is O in the office?' I ask breathlessly, signing in.

'She's in the dungeon. Checking the equipment. Do you need to see her?'

'Yes. Yes, I do.'

'She won't be long. Grab a coffee upstairs while you're waiting.'

'Cheers, I will.'

But I don't.

The café is almost empty, just me and the barista and a guy covered in tattoos eating cupcakes in the corner.

I order the coffee and take it to the table nearest the door to the private rooms. It's a bit of a blind spot, invisible from the bar area, tucked in a corner. I take two sips, wait for the barista to start messing about with his phone then sneak down to the dungeon.

Schoolroom, empty. Medical room, empty. Dungeon ...

I push the door and fit my eye to the crack.

I nearly run back upstairs.

O is completely naked, her arms cuffed to a wooden cross, her head thrown back, her spine rubbing against the varnished post in near ecstasy.

After my initial pang, my eye is drawn back to her. She looks so beautiful, so wanton, so desirable. Her legs are slightly parted, exposing her shaved pussy lips and the teeny-tiny tip of her clit, which is pierced, like her nipples. Even when I watched her fucking the other day, she didn't look this … rapt.

I feel guilty but I can't stop watching. My forehead nudges the door and it creaks, unexpectedly.

'Is that you, Mal?'

Her eyes have focused, snap, just like that, and she looks straight at me, expectantly.

I want to run, but my legs have gone. 'I'm so sorry,' I gabble, pushing the door. 'It's me. I didn't mean to spy. I just … I wanted to ask you something.'

Her eyes widen and she stares for a silent age. 'Rosie. Come over here.'

I look back, still contemplating escape, but there's no point now, so I walk over to her. What can she do to me with her arms strapped to the cross anyway?

'You can see how I'm fixed,' she drawls. 'Mal'll be here in a minute. He'll be interested to see you.'

I try to keep my eyes from dropping to her breasts and crotch. I feel a bit like a pervy old man must feel. But she's so gorgeous, all naked and spread-eagled there.

'I just wondered,' I say, feeling ineffably stupid, 'if you'd seen Dimitri at all this morning.' I pause. 'I can't get hold of him, you see,' I add helpfully.

'Ah, Dimitri,' she says, rolling his name around in her mouth like a fine wine. 'Isn't everyone trying to get hold of him?'

She seems to enjoy my anxiety. 'Are they? Really? Like who?'

'Oh, just people in general. He's such an attractive man, isn't he? Seems tragic to keep him all to yourself. A man like that has so much to offer the community.'

My admiration of her turns to dislike.

'That's rather up to him, isn't it?' I say tightly. 'I like this idea that community spirit involves whipping every backside that bares itself to you. Do you think the government would go for that idea? Beats the Big Society, doesn't it? So to speak.'

She laughs. 'You're an interesting girl too, Rosie. To be fair, a lot of the tops have their eyes on you. Including Mal.'

'Well, I'm not available. Except to Dimitri. Look, do you want me to undo those cuffs?' O is starting to look uncomfortable.

'No, it's fine. Mal won't thank you for it. I've orders to stay like this until he comes back. What you said about only being available to Dimitri though … are you sure he feels that way?'

'What do you mean?'

'He's a free spirit, Rosie. Don't you see that? He can't be caged by one person's jealousy or possessiveness. He needs his space.'

'You seem to know him very well.'

'We've spoken at length, every time he's booked a

room here. You can't hang on to a man like that. He's not for hanging on to. He's for experiencing and adoring and remembering all your life. But you can't expect to keep him.'

'What the hell have you been talking about? You sound like some kind of hippy dippy sixties song lyric.'

'Let's just say I'm a good reader of people.'

'Let's just say you're spouting all this crap because you want him for yourself.'

'I certainly wouldn't say no. But I wouldn't try to stifle him either, or keep him from making other people happy.'

'What about what makes *him* happy? Have you thought about that?'

'Have you?'

'Of course … I have.'

She catches the hesitation, a hesitation that comes of seeing him leave the building with Trixietots earlier. Does he want to spread himself around, for love as well as money? Have I just been the practice model, helping him hone his skills for the real deal?

I really didn't think so. I really thought there was something special between us. But what do I know?

'He wants to be a pro-dom. Does that sound like a one-woman man to you?'

'He needs money.'

'There are so many ways of earning money, my dear.

Being a pro-dom isn't the first one that springs to mind, is it?'

'Well, it's something he enjoys and he's good at it. It doesn't mean he wants to sleep around. In fact, he's said loads of times that he wouldn't have sex with his clients.'

'He's said that to *you*.'

'What, so he's told you different?'

'He doesn't need to. Actions speak louder than words.'

'What?' I leap up close to O, stretching on tiptoes so our noses almost touch. It's an act of aggression, and I wish I could stop myself, but once I've done it I can't seem to step back out of it. 'What the fuck do you mean by that?'

'What the fuck do *you* mean by threatening my partner?' The voice, cold and male, comes from the doorway.

I come to my senses and move back, subdued and close to tears. 'I'm sorry,' I mutter to Mal as he strides into the room. 'I didn't mean to get so worked up.'

'I suppose this is all about beloved Dimitri, is it?' he says. He sounds resigned, and a little bit pissed off. 'O, you know you can't have him, but it doesn't stop you from trying, does it?'

A tiny flicker of hope sparks up. I work hard at hanging on to it.

'She's obsessed with him,' he tells me. 'But he isn't obsessed with her. When that happens, you have to let it go. You know it, darling, don't you? But you won't be told.' He caresses her under the chin, then takes hold of a nipple and twists it.

I wince in sympathy.

She whimpers, 'But he's so pretty. I want him so much.'

'You can't have everything. You're spoiled enough as it is. Have you been telling tales to poor Rosie here? Is that why she got cross with you?'

'I didn't tell her anything that wasn't true.'

She gasps as he smacks the side of her breast, hard. I watch the flesh jiggle and sway.

'He's not yours, O. You can't be his. You're mine. Repeat it.'

'I'm yours, master.'

'That's right. You forget it too often, pet. I think you need a reminder.'

She smiles at that, a big wonky dirty smile, running her tongue along the top row of her teeth with lascivious glee.

'Please remind me, master.'

'I will. And, since Rosie here has been upset by your ridiculous crush, I think she should stay and watch.'

'If you think so, master.'

'I do. Is that all right with you, Rosie?'

'Well, I, er …'

'Take a seat.'

I still haven't had a chance to ask about Trixietots,

but Mal seems impossible to defy. He is the old-school dom, as opposed to Dimitri's odd and whimsical version, and he carries his air of authority with him at all times, like a gold-topped cane.

I sit down on the stage and watch while Mal unshackles O from the cross, giving her a moment to stretch her arms and rotate her wrists.

'I'm going to go for an old favourite, I think,' he says, going over to the wall and pulling away a piece of furniture that looks like a normal kitchen stool, apart from one thing: the long thick dildo erupting out of the seat like a rocket.

'Over here, my love,' says Mal, the words not menacing in themselves, but his tone pure evil.

O looks apprehensive, pouting at Mal as she crosses the floor. 'You're really going to make me ride it in front of Rosie?'

'Have you ever used one of these, Rosie?' Mal asks me, stroking the mountainous dildo.

'No.'

'Dimitri's missing a trick. Hop on, then.'

The last words are addressed to O, who looks sulkily away from me as she places her feet delicately on the low rungs of the stool, steadying herself with palms flat on the seat. To mount it properly, she has to first kneel above the giant protuberance and lower herself, slowly and with much wincing, down on to it. I watch transfixed as her lips stretch and the latex is slowly swallowed up inside her.

Once it is almost subsumed, she adjusts her legs, painstakingly, standing back on the rungs. This forces her into a position where she has to bend forwards at the waist, hands clasped on the seat in front of her, bottom pushed out.

'Doesn't she look nice?' purrs Mal.

She certainly looks obscene. Mal makes me examine her from every angle, so I see her strained face from the front, her penetrated profile, her wide open bum cheeks from the back.

'Now, ride. Ride it well. I'm going to use the whip.'

She begins to move herself up and down on the dildo. It looks laborious, her calves shaking and thighs straining with each up-and-down motion.

'Faster than that.' Mal selects a wicked-looking flogger and starts lashing it against her bottom. The whoosh and splat are enormously satisfying. O grunts with effort, every facial muscle contracted.

But I don't want to watch her face. I want to see her arse, jiggling up and down on the thick stalk, changing colour under the lash. I want to see what Dimitri might see.

I can't deny that it looks incredibly sexy. O's pert backside seems made for the whip and her slender body looks so fragile yet it must be so strong to keep up the frantic pace Mal seems to require. Her stamina impresses me as she races to the finish, but her criss-crossed rear impresses me even more. The redder and angrier it looks, the more I am turned on until I can hardly bear it, having to scrunch up my fists to keep my fingers away from my skirt hem.

Mal plies his flogger mercilessly, catching the tender spot at the top of O's thighs until she screams. Oh dear, I think, now he's gone too far and will have to stop, but then I realise that the scream is not inspired by pain, or only partially so.

O is coming, jolting back and forth, the scream breaking into a series of little whines while the whip falls again and again.

I don't know whether to pity or envy her. On the whole, the balance tips towards envy. Can I get Dimitri to do this to me?

Dimitri.

Where is he?

I turn to Mal, who is unbelting and unbuckling his leather trousers, preparing to release his stiff cock.

'Do you know where Dimitri is this morning?' I ask him.

He puts the whip away and moves around to the front of O, waiting for her to take him in her mouth before answering.

'No. Ah, that's good, O, that's very good.'

'I'll, um, be getting on then.'

'Must you? Stay if you want.'

'No, no, that's fine. Goodbye.'

O is feasting on Mal's cock, still connected to the dildo-stool, when I leave, not much the wiser.

On the one hand, I know that Dimitri hasn't been mixing it up with O – she has a crush on him, but that's all. But I know nothing about what he's doing with Trixietots, or where they are.

Lunchtime is coming up when I stagger back on to street level, workers pouring out of their offices and heading for the pubs and sandwich bars of the district. Wherever Dimitri and Trixietots are, looking for them will be like finding ants in an anthill. Really, I should just go back to the office and try to call him again.

But I can't. I just can't.

I find myself phoning my account manager and telling him I've just thrown up in the car park, must be some kind of bug, hopefully I'll be fine tomorrow and all that.

Then I take a purposeful right turn around the corner and commit to a fine-tooth-comb search of the entirety of the N1 postal area.

I only make it as far as the same pub we escaped to after that intriguing vision through the basement window of Kinky Cupcake. There, in a corner, sit Dimitri and Trixietots, both nursing tumblers of vodka. He has his arm around her and he's beaming away as if his smile is powered by the National Grid. She is fawning and blushing and pushing her knee up close to his.

That story about throwing up in the car park suddenly feels a whole lot more plausible.

I put my hand over my mouth, turn and run to the tube station.

* * *

Saturday comes.

There has been no contact between Dimitri and me over the preceding two days except a text from him vaguely referring to 'big news'. I didn't reply to it, unable to keep up the appearance of normality.

Today I will set him free. That's what the song says, isn't it? If you love somebody, set them free.

I am a human jitterbug as I walk slowly up the narrow street to Kinky Cupcake. This is going to be horrible, but it has to be done. Then I can meet Anton at the Laser Zone and bury myself in mindless pleasure-seeking for the rest of the weekend.

Dimitri is in the café, reading the sports pages of a newspaper while his coffee goes cold. At least Trixietots doesn't appear to be on the scene. I seat myself opposite him, rather than doing my usual thing of sliding in beside him for enthusiastic and somewhat bristly hello kisses.

He puts down the paper and grins the wolfish grin. 'Hey, baby,' he says, then his mouth slides to a mock-sad droop. 'You are OK? Not looking so happy.'

My lips do an annoying wobbling thing as I try to get the words out. Not the calm, firm effect I had hoped for at all.

'I just want you to know,' I open, everything pouring out in an uneven rush, 'that I don't expect anything from you.'

'What? I thought you expect me to whip you today?'

'That's not what I mean. I mean, I know what you're like. You don't have to pretend you like me as more than … than what you … I mean, if you don't really want me, that's fine. I think you'll make a wonderful dom. Thank you and goodbye.'

I rise on unsteady feet and stare desperately at the door. It looks miles away. My first attempt to hurl myself at it fails miserably, foiled by Dimitri lunging after me and catching hold of an upper arm. He spins me round to face him. I want to die. What a scene we're making!

'What?' he demands in a stunned whisper. 'What you are talking about? Come here. Sit down.'

'Very convincing. Just like a real dom.' So like a real dom, in fact, that I do exactly as I'm told.

'What is wrong? Rosie, you are shaking. Look, I get you a drink. Stay there.'

I contemplate making a break for it, but I can't bear

to sneak away from him. The thought of his mild shock and consternation when he returns to the table and finds me gone makes my heart weep. I think he does care for me on some level, even if it isn't the one I was hoping for.

He comes back with the richest possible hot chocolate, well, more a cream and marshmallow concoction with some hot chocolate included by the looks of things, and sets it down in front of me.

'Sugar,' he says, as if I'm supposed to grasp his meaning. 'You drink it. And you tell me what is the problem here. I did something to make you sad?'

'No. But you did something that showed me how things really are.'

'How things really are? How is that?'

'I got carried away. The S&M stuff is really intense – I suppose that made me think our relationship was also really intense.'

'Intense?'

'Full-on. Heavy. Um, very emotional. I don't know. Too much.'

'I scare you with what I do to you?'

'No, no. I'm not explaining myself very well. To do what we do, I had to trust you. And like you. A lot. And I suppose I thought you felt the same.'

'Stop, you think I don't like you a lot? Because that is not true. I like you a lot. A very lot.'

'That's nice. But it's not just me you like a lot, is it?'

He blinks at me, utterly bamboozled, or so he wants me to think. 'I am not understanding you.'

'I saw you with Trixietots. In the pub. All over her – your arms around her. And I don't mind! I really don't. You can shag who you like. But maybe it's time you went pro. Maybe you're ready now. Thanks for the experience, it was amazing, but –'

'Shut up!'

I am too shocked to speak. He sounds quite angry. Eyes from the other tables swivel in our direction.

He breathes in, stills himself, exhales. When he speaks again, his voice is low.

'You see me with Trixietots in the pub, right?'

I nod.

'So why you don't come and say hello?'

'I was … I thought you wouldn't want to see me, while you and she …'

'You mean you think me and Trixietots, we are lovers? Outside your back?'

'Behind my back. Well, yes. But you don't have any obligation to me.'

'Shush. You make a wrong … I don't know the word.'

'Decision? Conclusion?'

'Conclusion, I think. You decide I am lovers with Trixietots. But I am not.'

His voice is still controlled, but his hand gestures

aren't. His rattling bangles can be heard on the other side of the Thames, probably.

'Aren't you?'

'No.'

'But you will be? You want to be?'

An even more emphatic, 'No!'

'So?'

'Trixietots – her name is Louise actually – she is an agent. Agent for theatre.'

'Theatrical agent?'

'Yes. And she sign me. She find me work in a movie about economic immigrants. It start to film next month.'

I don't know what to say. 'Oh.'

He sniffs at me, mortally wounded. I feel like the jerkiest jerk since jerkdom was invented.

'I mean, congratulations. Wow. That's awesome news. I'm so pleased for you.'

'No more kitchen for me.'

'Fantastic. Well done.' I want to cry. I think I'm going to. 'I'm so sorry.' My voice cracks.

He pushes the hot chocolate towards me. 'Drink some.'

The marshmallows stick in my craw.

'One problem I have,' he continues, looking gloomily at the table. 'I need to make better my English. I have plan to ask you if you can help me. Evenings, maybe. But now, I don't know.'

'Oh,' I say again. My oh-saying skills are on fire today.

'You have bad idea of me. I have disappointment.'

'I don't – I never did. I just thought it was only fair to let you have some freedom. You're going to dominate all these strangers anyway. I don't have any claim on you.'

'I need to understand this, Rosie,' he said, leaning forwards. 'You are saying that you like me a lot. This is right?'

'God, yes. I really do. I …' No, better not say that. Hold back.

'There is fire, yes, for you and me? The sex, it is very good?'

'You know it is.'

'And we both are enjoying the kink?'

'Absolutely.'

'So, you like me in all this way. But you also want me to fuck other girls and leave you alone? This is what you are saying?'

'No. I'm not really saying that. I only said that because I thought that was what you wanted. Is it?'

'Not at all. I want you.'

The sudden declaration takes what little wind I have left from my sails.

'Really? As a submissive? A sex partner?'

'Of course.' He rolls his eyes. 'But more than that too. I mean, you know, we go to a movie and so on. Meet my friends, I meet your friends.'

'You never really said …'

'No, because, look at me, Rosie.'

I do. It's no hardship, but he seems to think he gestures towards something less than desirable. Weird.

'What I have got to give you? I am poor, I am foreign, I am man who has nothing.'

'I've never seen you that way. Not at all. To me, you've got everything.'

At last the anger seems to burn off and a genuine smile breaks out from behind the clouds. 'See, that is why you are special to me. And you like me for myself.'

'I think Trixietots and O might do too, though,' I say, unable to stop the mischievous thought tripping off my tongue. 'To be fair.'

'No, no, they like me because they think I am a dom.'

'You *are*.'

'Thank you. I don't think I can be professional though.'

'Really? Why not?'

'Like you say, to do this acts is very emotional. It works for me and for you because we love each other.'

My heart swells. That word. And now he's said it, yes, it's out there and it can't ever go back in.

'I think I can't do it to a girl I don't love.'

'You only hurt the one you love.' The thought is ridiculously cheering. I find myself smiling again.

'That seems a little bit mad, yes? But I feel it in my heart.'

'Me too.'

It's as if a loud, stormy movement of music has given way to peaceful harmony. We are back. We are lovers. We love each other.

'So, Rosie,' he says, after spending a moment clasping my hands in his.

'Yes?'

'You have a bad idea of me and you try to break up with me. I don't think this is good.'

There is a particular tilt of his head, a particular look in his eye that hints at what is coming. I shiver and squirm in my seat, my throat suddenly dry.

'I'm very sorry,' I say softly, adding, even more quietly, 'sir.'

He shakes his head. 'Apology is good, but not good enough. And, how lucky, I have booked the dungeon. Come with me.'

Chapter Nine

I'm not dressed for it, not today.

If I hadn't been full of the resolve to end things with Dimitri, I might have gone for a skirt, stockings, something he could flip up or tear off with the greatest of ease, but I am wearing jeans and a fleece-lined hoodie. Not appropriate dungeon-wear at all.

Somehow this skews my experience. I feel like a tourist stumbling on to a film set instead of a submissive. Or perhaps I'm still dazed from all the revelations. Either way, I can't quite connect with my kink.

Dimitri, having walked me down the staircase with a hand on my shoulder, lets go of me to conduct a thorough search of the implement store.

'What is best,' he mutters under his breath, 'for a

girl who has no faith in her master?'

Her master. That does it. The hoodie and jeans melt away from my consciousness and I feel naked, small and ashamed. And very turned on.

'What do you think, Rosie?' he asks, twisting his neck to look over at me. 'What do you deserve?'

'Isn't that your decision?'

'Not today.'

What do I deserve? And what does he mean by this question? Is it just a BDSM-flavoured way of asking me what I want? Or does he actually want me to quantify the seriousness of my transgression? How bad is it – is it cane-bad or just flogger-bad? I know the answer before I finish the question.

'The cane,' I murmur. Today I want to feel it. I want the pain. I want the afterburn. I want to feel completely punished and completely owned and completely loved. I can't say why, but I know that only the cane will do this for me today.

'The cane? You are sure?'

He selects one from the cabinet – a long slender stick of rattan, curving at the end. He straightens up and whips it through the air. The sound makes me shiver and swoon together.

'Don't be scared,' he says. 'Well, yes, be scared if you want, but don't be scared because I have no experience. I practise with this. I use a cushion. I am quite an expert now.'

He moves towards me like a musketeer with a duelling sword, pointing the cane at me until the tip of it reaches underneath my chin. He taps it gently, forcing my neck to tilt back and my eyes to reach up to his.

When I see how solemn, how serious he looks, I try to swallow. It takes a while.

'Don't never do this to me again, Rosie,' he says in a low, soft voice. 'You think you have a problem with me, you tell me. Always. Yes?'

'Yes.'

'Right.' He moves the cane, outlining my jaw with it, passing its cold smooth wood over my cheeks, down to my neck, around my shoulder, then he taps it firmly against a hip. 'OK. You want for me to punish you. I am ready. Turn around and bend over.'

'But I'm still wearing –'

'I don't want no argument. Do it.'

I spin around and consider how best to arrange myself. It's hard to maintain this posture with nothing to hold on to and he has offered no chair, no spanking bench, none of the usual accoutrements. If I grab my ankles, will that support me? I try it. It feels sustainable. I am aware of how tightly the denim is stretched across my bum now. Suddenly it doesn't feel as thick or protective any more.

'My God, your ass looks nice this way,' says Dimitri.

I flinch and almost fall forwards when he puts a hand

on one cheek, running it over the taut material, squeezing and patting. The seam that runs between my thighs presses tight into my knickers, lodging itself between my pussy lips. They feel hot and itchy. I want to rub.

'I give you two strokes on your jeans,' decrees Dimitri. 'Just so you get a feel.'

He removes his hand and steps back and to the side a little. He taps the cane against my bottom in a steady, almost soothing rhythm, then there is a swoosh as he draws it back.

I need to savour my last milliseconds as an uncaned person. I need to hold this non-pain in my heart and memory, because it will be over so soon, so soon ...

With a swish and a snap, my uncaned life is over. The moment of impact makes me cry out, more from shock than pain, though pain is certainly involved. It's a sweet, sharp pain that seeps right through the fabric and draws a line beneath it, setting my skin alight.

'How is that?'

'It hurts.'

'Too much?'

I consider this while my hair swings in my face and my toes curl. 'No.'

'Right.' And there's the second, straight away, a little lower than the first, throbbing against the denim so I imagine it as a stripe of flashing neon. 'You are thinking about how sorry you are?'

'I'm thinking about how much it hurts!'

'Of course. But also?'

'I'm sorry. Really sorry. It really hurts! Over jeans. God knows what it's like –'

'Take them down.'

I exhale shudderingly, then release my ankles and stand straight. My arse still feels like it's on fire, and the act of lowering the rough denim over the two burning lines only exacerbates the effect. I sneak a sideways peek at Dimitri. He looks grim. I bite my lip and let the jeans crumple down below my knees.

The cane prods at my cotton knickers.

'Back down now. Two more.'

I dare to look at him again, hoping to convey sincere regret and have my sentence commuted. But if it was, would I be happy with that? I don't think I would. There's perversity in perversion.

Anyway, there's nothing in his face to suggest he's about to drop the cane and review the tariff. My hands and ankles meet again, my bum thrust out, infinitely more vulnerable without its tough casing. The knickers are of serviceable cotton, rather washed out and thinner than they should be. They won't protect much.

The swish and snap fill my ears for a third time. This time I can't maintain my position. I leap up and put a hand on my arse, rubbing it while I catch my breath.

'Oh God,' I say. 'It's too much.'

'You want to stop?'

I consider it, then shake my head. 'No.' My voice is a bit wobbly, coming from somewhere deep in my head, but it seems to know what it means. 'Not yet.'

'Why you are on your feet then? Get back down or I give you extra.'

It hurts so much that I don't even realise how tightly clenched all my muscles are until he taps my thigh with the cane and orders me to relax.

'It's horrible,' I whinge, though I guess he's gathered as much. 'I hate it.'

'Uh-huh. And it's what you deserve, yes?'

His implacability in the face of my pathetic whimperings impresses me, reminds me of the heat between my legs, which rages just as intensely as the hardening welts on my bum. A presentiment of how extraordinary the sex is going to be after this steels me and I await the fourth stroke with meek acceptance.

It wrings a sob from me, and I fall forwards onto my knees and lay my head on my forearms, lamenting my fate so hard that surely his heart will soften. 'Ow, ow, ow, ow, it's horrible, I hate it, ohhhhh.'

But still no plea to stop.

'So much drama! I thought it is me who is the actor. But you will get up, please, or there is more strokes for you.'

I can't disobey him. Even though I know what's coming

next, and every pore of my skin – especially those on my rear – dreads it, I haul myself to my feet again, keeping my hands over my face.

'You take down your panties now.'

I give myself a moment to build up to it.

'You take them down now or I do it. If I do it, there is more punishment.'

'You're so *fierce*,' I moan. 'You're harsh.'

I lower the knickers gingerly. Part of them sticks to the sore patches and I have to suck in a breath while I peel the cotton off. They float down my legs to join the bunched jeans around my feet. Now I have nothing at all between my poor painful bottom and his evil cane.

'Oh, this is a good job.' He sounds absolutely delighted with himself. His fingers alight on the fizzing welts, drifting along them admiringly. 'Good spaces, you know. Very straight. Very clear. This must hurt a lot.'

'Didn't you realise?'

'You are giving me backchat? Do you really want to do that?'

'No, sir. Sorry, sir.'

'Back down.' He holds the hand against my bottom, keeping me steady. 'And this is the last two, right? But you tell me you are sorry after each one. And you say my name. You say, "Sorry, Dimitri." You can do this?'

'I think so.'

For the flicker of a moment I wonder why he doesn't

want 'Sorry, sir,' or the more classic 'Thank you, sir.' And then I realise why – it's because this isn't really a BDSM 'scene'. This is something more personal, something more intimate. It's a bonding experience, the establishment of a new order in our relationship. My heart swells with emotion.

And then my bum swells with awful, gigantic, white-hot hideous pain.

I almost think I'm going to throw up, but the worst of it passes, leaving the fierce after-effects to do their stuff. *I can't take this, I can't take this, I can't take this.*

But I will take this.

I will take it for him.

My head clears and I remember to think again.

'Sorry, Dimitri.' My tongue slurs it and it comes out very, very quietly.

'I don't hear you.'

'Sorry,' I say with more of an effort. 'Dimitri.'

'Yes, I think you are. One more. Be brave. You are brave, Rosichka.'

He puts a hand on my spine and strokes it up and down. My breathing calms. His fingers press into my shoulder blades and neck, unknotting the gathering tension.

'Just one,' he whispers.

He steps away again, big boots on flagstones, and I make a gargantuan effort not to knot myself back up immediately.

I can't, I can, I can't, I can, I can't, I will.

I do.

Oh God, it's the worst one yet and I scream it out, jumping up and clutching my bum as if it's on fire, which it well might be.

'Jesus!'

'No, no. Dimitri. Say it.'

He takes hold of me by the shoulders, pulling me into his chest, letting me sob into it for a moment or two. Everything is shaking, every single bit of me, even my eyes. He is still and strong and the shaking ends before long, though my legs still aren't quite up to par by the time I find my voice.

'Sorry, Dimitri.'

His lips are on the top of my head, kissing my hair. 'That's hard for you.'

'Very. Really very painful indeed. But I wanted to take it, for you.'

'Hard for me also. I almost stop.'

'I'm glad you didn't though.'

'I got afraid you will hate me. But if I start, I must finish.'

'I could never hate you.'

'I keep say to myself, wait for her to say stop. But it is very hard, you know. To hurt somebody you love. Even if you know they want it.'

I remove my face from his chest and regard him with interest. 'You didn't enjoy it?'

He wrinkles his nose. 'Well, yes. I like it from visual point of view, you know. It looks good. It feels good. But scary.'

'Scary, yeah. Do you think it would be scary if you were doing it to a client?'

'No, not at all. Only because it's you, you know.'

'Yes. I know. You didn't find it sexy then?'

'I don't say that.'

He winks at me and puts a hand over the hottest part of my bottom, patting it. Now that I know there are no more strokes coming, I am growing to love the pain, embrace its radiating throb as it courses through me. He gave it to me; it is precious.

Our lips meet and we kiss a heartfelt apology to one another. All is equal again. It's a fresh start, sealed with lips. And tongues.

Somewhere in the middle of it, he starts pushing me into a backwards shuffle, my feet moving in tiny steps, restricted by the jeans and knickers around my ankles.

I meet an obstacle, reaching to the backs of my knees, and I tumble backwards, landing with a gasp and an ouch on my bottom on a kind of leather divan fitted with wrist and ankle straps. It's the bondage bed.

Dimitri rolls on top of me, still kissing, his fingers pushing into my hair from the sides of my face, his pelvis grinding into mine. The cold leather soothes my cane marks for a heavenly second, then they start to hurt as

Dimitri jolts my body up and down. I want this pain, though. I want to feel it, along with the passion and the pleasure. The way they mix and spill into each other drives me to a level of need I never used to reach.

He releases my head and my mouth and props himself on his elbows, breathing down fast as he stares into my face. 'I need to fuck you,' he announces.

'Can I go on top?' I ask, fearing the moment I have to remove my welts from the sticky leather after a bout of sweaty intense sex.

'No,' he says, treating me to a swift nip of the lower lip. 'I want you to feel it. All the time I am fucking you, I want you to know that you were caned by me. Right?'

'Oh. Right. OK then.' I submit. It makes it even better that he refused my request. I am actively submitting and it feels amazing.

He rears up and removes the jeans and knickers, which allows him to open my legs with his knees and crouch back down over me, unzipping his own trousers. He is hard. His cock slips and slides inside my pussy lips, coating itself with my juices while the whole of my lower body pulses with heat from my caned bottom.

'You tell me when you are close,' he says, sitting back up to deal with the condom. 'Will you do that?'

'Yes.' Looking up at him, I think he could ask me anything right now and get the same response. *Yes, Dimitri, yes, yes, yes.*

'Don't forget.' He bears down and then he is in me. My bottom shifts on the leather, the lower portion slightly raised, entailing the reawakening of some very sore spots. I gasp with pain and moan with pleasure, one after the other.

'Does that hurt?' he asks, sinking in until I am full and stretched underneath him.

'A bit. I like it though.'

'I know. So look at me. Don't shut your eyes. I want you to look at me all the time I fuck you.'

It's more difficult than it sounds; easier than the time he took me up the arse, but only slightly. I feel he's trying to read every hidden, secret thought through my eyes, and succeeding. He knows I love this, to be fucked raw, to be used and dominated and beaten and mastered, and he needs me to know that he knows it. God, it's hard to admit to, but I have to do it. I have to be honest with him. If there's one thing I've learned today, it's that.

I look at him as he thrusts and I know he is seeing every shameful fantasy and every kinky urge that has ever crossed my mind. I can't hide any of it. Sometimes it gets too much and I want to turn my face away, but he catches my cheek with a finger and pushes me back into place every time. On my third thwarted attempt at mind-reading avoidance, I am climbing, heading up, near the point of orgasm and I know he can see it, so I'd better admit it.

'I'm close,' I whisper.

'I see that.' He stops, holds himself stock-still, biting his lip.

'Oh, don't stop, please.' I rotate my pelvis, trying to urge him back on track.

He pulls out.

I sit up, on one elbow, fighting my way back, reaching out for him. My tender bottom doesn't like this move and I hiss with sudden pain, but I have to get him back inside me.

'No, no,' he says. 'On your knees now.'

He turns me over, putting me on all fours. In one way, I am grateful for the opportunity this gives me to hide my face from him. In another, I'm not.

'Oh, look, look, look at this,' he croons behind me, smoothing his palms over my bottom. 'So pretty. OK, we do it this way now.'

Gloriously, he is back inside me, a good hard shove until his flat stomach meets my curving arse cheeks, adding to the heat that hasn't even begun to recede yet.

A groan of appreciation falls from my lips. This feels too good, indecently, obscenely good. His hands on my hips, then one clutching a big hank of my hair and tugging on it as he rides me, his skin on mine, banging into it, making the cane marks throb anew. It's a wild conjunction of every sensation and I surf it joyously until the moment nears again. Must I tell him again? Couldn't I keep it a secret?

'I'm close,' I mewl, a mite sulkily, dreading another withdrawal.

'Good, that's good.'

He keeps going.

Yes, that's good! I agree wholeheartedly.

I am laughing with delight when the wave crests, bathing in it, letting it wash all over me from my beaded brow to my curled-up toes, paying special attention to that sweet rear sting.

I say some words that don't make sense, might as well be the Russian ones he is coming out with now, as he jolts, in, in, in, hard, giving me his all.

We fall, slack-jawed and spent, together on the leather.

'I do love you,' I tell him. Is it the first time? Have I said it before? I can't even remember.

'I know, of course.' He yawns. 'And for me too.'

I am still wearing the fleece-lined flipping hoody. No wonder I'm so hot. It clings to my skin almost as tightly as he does.

'It doesn't seem fair,' I say sleepily, 'that you can read my thoughts when I can't read yours.'

'You can't?'

'No, of course not. They're in Russian. I don't speak a word of Russian.'

He laughs. 'I teach you. But you help me with English also.'

'Deal.'

We must have fallen asleep like that.

The next thing I know, there's a loud knocking on the dungeon door and O's voice, sounding very quiet and far away, asking us if we're done in here.

At first it seems like part of a dream, as does Dimitri's solid warmth beside and around me but, as my wits slowly sharpen, I realise I am really lying half dressed on a bondage bed in a dungeon with the mother of all sore bottoms.

Dimitri mutters in Russian, then shouts, 'You wait a minute, yes?' at the door.

He turns to me. 'I am sorry,' he says. 'I don't plan to sleep. I wanted to put the cream on you.'

For a fuzzy moment I think this is a euphemism, then, when he reaches down and pulls a tub out of his jeans pocket, I realise what he means.

'Oh! That's a nice thought. We can't, though, can we? Time's up.'

'Ah, she can wait. Turn over on your belly, yes?'

I hesitate for a moment, looking over at the door. I don't really want to see O again. I feel there's a certain *froideur* between us after that scene earlier in the week.

But Dimitri rubbing lotion on my poor stinging bottom … well, that's too good to turn down. I roll over and rest my head happily on my arms.

He slathers on the ointment in generous whorls, covering each stiff welt in moisturising balm. The smell of it is gorgeous, the feeling of it on my skin even more so, especially administered with Dimitri's magic touch.

'What's up? Do you need some help?'

We both snort gently at O's well-meaning offer.

'We're fine. Just give us a minute.'

'I have some clients here with me. They've booked for ten minutes ago. Dimitri, please can we come in?'

His fingertips glide along the lines between my cane marks like skaters.

'Two minutes,' he says.

'Oh, I can't wait for you, whatever you're up to. I'm coming in.'

'No!' I squeal, but the key is turning in the lock.

'Hey!' exclaims Dimitri, hurriedly capping the tub and making a lunge for his jeans.

'Look, I'm sorry.' O stands in the doorway. I am too late to even think about getting my knickers and jeans back on. I slump on the bondage bed, imagining her eyes – and those of the other clients – taking in my sheeny-shiny stripy arse. 'You booked for one hour and … What lovely work!' She waltzes over, cooing in rapture.

I hear Dimitri zip himself up and sniff. 'Thank you. You must not rush an artist.'

A stifled giggle escapes me at his grandiose tone, despite my conspicuous position.

'Oh, I quite agree. And this would make such a lovely photograph. You could give lessons, Dimitri. Would you be interested in leading a session on corporal punishment?'

'Corporal? This is something concerning the army, no?'

'Oh, no, no. It's another name for the spanking fetish, my dear. Though of course, when I was younger, it existed in the vanilla world too. Please excuse my dreadful manners – I should really introduce you.'

She makes a lengthy meal of explaining who her clients are, while I lie in several kinds of agony, avoiding showing my face throughout.

'And this is his submissive, Rosie. Are you going to say hello, Rosie?'

I muffle something into the leather padding, but Dimitri's hand on my hair, tugging at it, suggests I won't be allowed to get away with this.

'I think perhaps she's indisposed,' says the male client with a self-conscious chuckle.

'She can speak,' says Dimitri grimly.

I raise my head, twist my neck and mutter a greeting to the intrigued couple. They look sympathetic.

'That must hurt a lot,' the woman remarks.

'In a word, yes.'

'But without pain, no pleasure,' says the man.

'Sometimes.'

'I'm sorry,' says Dimitri. 'We are overstaying. Rosie, get dressed now.'

Any hope I foster that the three extraneous people in this room will avert their eyes is quickly dashed as I hop about looking for knickers and jeans. While they chat amongst themselves, they keep their gazes fixed on me. O winces in sympathy when I pull the knickers over my sore bottom, and the others join in when I torture myself by putting my jeans back on. Why the hell didn't I wear a skirt and hold-ups? These jeans might be heading for the charity shop.

Finally the ordeal ends and we leave the new clients to their playtime, following O up the stairs to the office.

'You know,' says O, stopping us in our tracks while we collect coats and bags from the small cloakroom in the lobby, 'I was serious when I said you should run a class. Are you interested at all?'

As usual, she is addressing Dimitri and ignoring me. My hackles rise.

'Not really,' I say, enjoying her eye-rolling at what she assumes to be my misunderstanding.

'I was asking Dimitri. He's the dom.'

'Are you saying submissives' opinions don't matter?'

'Of course not. I'm one myself, don't forget.'

'So the opinions of people you find attractive matter? Is that it?'

Dimitri is within an ace of winking at me. He puts a hand on my shoulder, but he makes no move to shut me up.

'It was just an idea.' She sounds really huffy now. I wonder if my membership is about to be revoked.

'We like this place,' I continue. 'Don't think we don't. We love it. We have wonderful times here and we appreciate everything you and Mal do for the kinkster community. Thank you. But I don't think I'm ready for public scenes yet. I'm not saying I never will be. But I'm not yet.'

'And I don't do scene without Rosie,' adds Dimitri, completing the explanation. 'We thank you very much.'

'Of course.' O tries to look cool about it, but it's obvious she's not. 'Everyone has their own comfort zone. I hope yours might expand in time.'

'It's possible,' says Dimitri. 'Good afternoon.'

We run down the stairs hand in hand. I don't think I've ever felt this exhilarated, amazing, blissful. And sore, of course, but that just makes it even better. We burst through the door and cannon straight into Anton.

'Watch it, geezer ... Rosie!'

It's lucky there aren't too many flies about because our combined open mouths would surely trap a few.

'Ahhhhhhello,' I say.

Dimitri holds out a bangly hand. 'Good afternoon, I am Dimitri Zacharov, you are friend of Rosie?'

Anton, his glance passing rapidly between us as if he is watching a frenzied tennis rally, puts out an uncertain hand. 'Er, yeah, Anton. Anton Smallbridge. Rosie?'

'So where are you off to?' I ask breezily. 'Laser Zone? Sorry I couldn't make it.'

'Yeah, 'cos you were in there. What the fuck?'

'You have a problem?' Dimitri's tone could be construed as menacing.

'Actually, bro, I do. I was supposed to be meeting Rosie half an hour ago at Laser Zone. But it looks like she's been in there with you. Any explanations gratefully received.'

'Look, why don't we go for a drink round the corner?' I steer the pair of them across the flats to the pub.

'So what is that place?' Anton's first question is a tricky one. After all, we aren't supposed to share the secret.

'It's a club. A private members-only club.'

He stares at me. 'How long have you been a member?'

'A few weeks.' I'm uncomfortable and I look for Dimitri's hand to hold on to.

'So all that time you were pretending to spy on it –'

'I know. I wasn't honest with you. But the managers don't like you to tell people.'

'Why? What kind of club is it? Illegal?' He points at Dimitri. 'Illegal immigrants?'

'Hey, I am legal,' he responds. 'I pay taxes.'

'Yeah, but who are you? And how do you know Rosie?'

'Rosie is my girlfriend.'

'But what ... when ...?' Anton flounders to a messy halt.

I take a deep breath. 'I met Dimitri outside the club last month. By chance, we managed to wangle an invitation from a member, so we decided to check it out. It's a, a, a BDSM club.'

There. I've said it.

Anton frowns for a second, then stares. 'What, like, bondage and all that?'

'Yes, but please don't tell anyone. It's completely private. Nobody must know.'

'Why not? It's not against the law, is it? Or do they actually kill each other in there?'

'No, they just prefer to keep it quiet, that's all.'

Anton thinks about this for a moment, drinking deep of his pint. 'You could have told me,' he says. He sounds very hurt. 'And you could have told me you had a boyfriend. Then I wouldn't have … you know. Shit. I'm a twat.'

'I'm sorry.'

'Why you don't tell him about me?' Now Dimitri sounds pissed off too. Marvellous.

'Because it was too complicated. And I didn't know for sure that you thought about me like that. I wasn't sure you didn't just think of us as play partners.'

'Well, we have sorted this out. But you let him think he has a chance with you. Why did you do that?'

'I didn't! Did I? I don't know. I thought we were friends. It's OK to have friends, isn't it?'

'Look at him.' Dimitri flaps a hand in Anton's direction. 'He is so very sad now. You crush his hopes.'

'Get lost.' Anton banged his pint glass on the table. 'I'm over it. I don't need your pity, bro.'

'Oh, don't fight,' I urge, conscious of the interest wafting in our direction from other tables. 'Look, whatever I did wrong, I'm sorry. Anton, if I ever gave you the impression I wanted to be more than friends, I didn't mean it. I really hope this isn't going to impact on our friendship.'

He makes me wait. I sip nervously at my wine.

'So which one of you's the dom?' he asks eventually.

Dimitri and I chime in together. 'I am.' 'He is.'

'Right. You should have told me you like to get spanked, Rosie. I'd have helped you out.'

Dimitri's eyes narrow. This might not be the best line of conversation. 'I hate to disappoint, but the only man who spanks Rosie is me.'

'I get that. I don't have to like it though. Shit, I wish I'd known what you were into. Maybe I could have –'

'You're interested in BDSM?'

'Yeah, a bit. I've watched some stuff on the internet now and again. Quite like the leather and rubber and all that.'

My chance to make amends leaps out and smacks me round the face. Just as well I enjoy it. 'Do you want me to get you an introduction?'

'What, to join the club? Could you do that?'

'I think so. Could I, Dimitri?'

'If you ask Mal. You and O, not so friendly right now.'

'Or you could ask. They think the sun shines out of your backside.'

'You're the one with the shining backside, no?'

'Shhh.' My face flares with embarrassment. Despite announcing my predilections to Anton, I still feel acutely coy about the whole thing. Even more so when Anton joins in with Dimitri's teasing laughter.

'I'd pay bloody good money to watch,' says Anton. 'I don't know if I could take part, though. I'd feel a bit weird. I don't think I've got the moves.'

'The moves are easy to learn,' says Dimitri. 'Trust me. If you like, I teach you.'

Oh God. Anton is going to attend Dimitri's dom school. This might be the most embarrassing drink of my life.

'You know, I might take you up on that. But let's get the club thing sorted first, yeah?'

It seems the least I can do.

'OK.' I put down my glass and haul myself to my feet. 'Let's go and talk to Mal.'

Chapter Ten

'Are you comfortable to sit?'

Three days after the caning, my bottom and wood still lack a fundamental affinity, and these schoolroom chairs are the worst.

'Here.' Dimitri unwraps a scarf from his neck and makes a show of laying it out on the seat for me.

Anton and some of the other audience members look on with intrigued amusement.

'Stop making a show of me.' I am drenched in embarrassment as I perch carefully on the blended wool silk. Dimitri puts an arm around my waist, pulling his chair right up close to mine.

'What did you do to her?' Anton wants to know, but before he can get an answer the demonstrators march onto the podium and the room hushes.

Mal is the teacher tonight, and Trixietots is his willing and able assistant. She is wearing a tiny plaid mini-kilt and over-the-knee socks; her breasts almost burst out of the tightly buttoned white shirt she is wearing, with obligatory skew-whiff tie.

We are here, rather unnecessarily in Dimitri's case, to watch a caning masterclass. I think Anton should really start with Spanking 101, but he insisted on enrolling for this one as his first taste of the delights of Kinky Cupcake, so here we are.

We watch as Trixietots demonstrates every kind of bending-over stance imaginable and Mal explains the benefits of each. With each new pose he invites an audience member to come up and smack her knicker-clad bum – Anton is first to be picked and returns from the rostrum grinning like a lunatic.

'This is my kind of school, innit,' he says, reseating himself.

Next Mal talks us through a variety of different canes. Every thickness, every material is represented and, once he has finished talking, he has Trixietots pull down her knickers and take a stroke from each.

She is amazingly controlled. I flinch with each stroke, expecting her to jump up or scream or clutch her bum, but she doesn't do any of it.

'How does she keep so still?' I whisper to Dimitri.

'I don't know. I will make you keep still next time. I will get you as still as her.'

I shudder, sure it can't be possible, and hoping 'next time' might be a long way in the future.

I watch each line materialise along the ample cheeks of her bum, crossing the cleft, until she has a neat grid of strokes. I shift in my chair, wishing I was her, which is madness, of course, because I hate the cane. But it is so very, very sexy.

'This is how the marks look, you see, when they are fresh.' Mal runs the tip of a cane across each newly laid welt. 'They fade with time, or some might present as bruising, especially from the heavier implements. In fact, I think there's someone in this room with some older marks.'

I suck in a breath. Mal looks directly at me.

'Rosie? A few days ago, wasn't it? Would you be very, very kind and show us how they look now?'

'Oh, I, I don't know.'

I try to collapse myself into as tiny a ball as I can, flamingly aware that everyone in the room (a) knows I am sitting on a caned bottom (b) expects to be able to get a good look at it.

'Maybe if Dimitri comes up with you?'

'Come on,' he whispers in my ear. 'You are brave. You can do it.'

If he wants me to do it, I'll do it. His word makes all the difference.

I let him help me to my feet and lead me to the stage, avoiding all eyes, especially Anton's. I won't have to face them anyway. It's not my face they want to see.

I am placed beside Trixietots, who is still bent over a chair. Dimitri runs a hand along my spine, pushing me gently into a forward inclination, less pronounced than Trixie's, but still making my neck and head droop down. He keeps one hand rubbing my back while the other lifts my skirt, so slowly and softly that I almost don't notice. I shut my eyes, blocking out the harsh schoolroom light. Cold air trickles up the backs of my thighs. Their eyes are on my thighs. I goose pimple all over.

He is so careful, so delicate when he pulls the knickers down. He doesn't brush the marks, doesn't even touch them. Once the elastic is safely at thigh level, he straightens up and holds me in position with his palms on my shoulders, thumbs massaging my neck.

A confusion of thoughts swirls in my head. Everyone is looking at my arse, but Dimitri's hands feel so nice, and it doesn't matter, they all do this kind of thing anyway, and all the subs will be envious of me and want Dimitri to do the same to them, especially the straight women and gay men.

It's good. This is my kink. I own it. I should enjoy it. I'm wet.

I hope they can't see it.

Mal drones on over my head about the colour and the distinctive pattern and all that, ending up with a fulsome compliment to Dimitri on his technique.

'You have a great skill,' he says, 'though I'm not sure Rosie would agree. Eh, Rosie?'

I shake the pleasurable blur from my head, cursing him for making me participate. 'He knows what he's doing,' I mutter.

'He does! I guess you've been behaving yourself ever since, eh?'

'I guess,' I grouch amid knowing laughter from the audience.

'Thank you, ladies, your assistance is much appreciated. Now, are there any questions?'

Trixietots and I cover our behinds and leave the stage.

'Hey, do you and your new friend fancy a drink upstairs afterwards?' she asks brightly. 'I don't think the pub will let me in dressed like this.'

'I don't think so,' says Dimitri, heading for the door.

'Aw, why not?'

'I have to discuss Rosie's bad behaviour with her.'

'Eh, what?' I protest.

'You think this is a good way to behave?' He raises an eyebrow at me. 'Rosie, you just show your ass to the whole room. I am very disappointed. Now let's go home and I will think of your punishment.'

He is evil, yet the best kind of evil. The kind I want.

'Lucky girl,' says Trixietots wistfully, as we walk out of the room.

She's not wrong.

THE SILVER CHAIN – PRIMULA BOND

Good things come to those who wait…

After a chance meeting one evening, mysterious entrepreneur Gustav Levi and photographer Serena Folkes agree to a very special contract.

Gustav will launch Serena's photographic career at his gallery, but only if Serena agrees to become his companion.

To mark their agreement, Gustav gives Serena a bracelet and silver chain which binds them physically and symbolically. A sign that Serena is under Gustav's power.

As their passionate relationship intensifies, the silver chain pulls them closer together. But will Gustav's past tear them apart?

A passionate, unforgettable erotic romance for fans of *50 Shades of Grey* and Sylvia Day's *Crossfire Trilogy*.

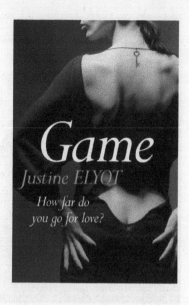

GAME – JUSTINE ELYOT

The stakes are high, the game is on.

In this sequel to Justine Elyot's bestselling *On Demand*, Sophie discovers a whole new world of daring sexual exploits.

Sophie's sexual tastes have always been a bit on the wild side – something her boyfriend Lloyd has always loved about her.

But Sophie gives Lloyd every part of her body except her heart. To win all of her, Lloyd challenges Sophie to live out her secret fantasies.

As the game intensifies, she experiments with all kinds of kinks and fetishes in a bid to understand what she really wants. But Lloyd feature in her final decision? Or will the ultimate risk he takes drive her away from him?

Find out more at www.mischiefbooks.com

POWER PLAY – CHARLOTTE STEIN

Now she's the boss, everything that once seemed forbidden is possible…

Meet Eleanor Harding, a woman who loves to be in control and who puts Anastasia Steele in the shade.

When Eleanor is promoted, she loses two very important things: the heated relationship she had with her boss, and control over her own desires.

She finds herself suddenly craving something very different – and office junior, Ben, seems like just the sort of man to fulfil her needs. He's willing to show her all of the things she's been missing – namely, what it's like to be the one in charge.

Now all Eleanor has to do is decide…is Ben calling the kinky shots, or is she?

Find out more at www.mischiefbooks.com

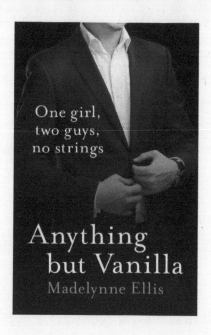

ANYTHING BUT VANILLA
MADELYNNE ELLIS

One girl, two guys, no strings.

Kara North is on the run. Fleeing from her controlling fiancé and a wedding she nev
wanted, she accepts the chance offer of refuge on Liddell Island, where she soon
catches the eye of the island's owner, erotic photographer Ric Liddell.

But pleasure comes in more than one flavour when Zachary Blackwater, the charmi
ice-cream vendor also takes an interest, and wants more than just a tumble in the su

When Kara learns that the two men have been unlikely lovers for years, she becom
obsessed with the idea of a threesome.

Soon Kara is wondering how she ever considered committing herself to just one ma

Find out more at www.mischiefbooks.com